Numbed

G. A. GUZMAN

Numbed

How to fall in love or get lost in the process.

"I've never had a problem with
drugs. I've had problems with the
police."

Keith Richards

TABLE OF CONTENTS

CHAPTER 1 — 11

CHAPTER 2 — 18

CHAPTER 3 — 39

CHAPTER 4 — 54

CHAPTER 5 — 66

CHAPTER 6 — 77

CHAPTER 7 — 90

CHAPTER 8 — 100

CHAPTER 9 — 111

CHAPTER 10 — 120

CHAPTER 11 — 134

CHAPTER 12 — 144

CHAPTER 13 — 154

CHAPTER 14   165

CHAPTER 15   175

Chapter 1

Reality snaps back into focus, and as I'm in the front seat of my car, I see a dozen drilling eyeballs staring into the windshield. What time is it? The dashboard clock reads 8:45 a.m. Each digit is a piercing reminder that I'm already out of sync with this day. I do not know these people, so their gaze means nothing to me; more pressing sensations grip me. The leather seats cool against my skin, blonde hair moves rhythmically below my sight line, and the remnants of last night surround me: an empty flask peeking out from under the seat, the faint stink of booze, and a rush of adrenaline kicks in. The drunkenness fades as I start to reckon with the scene. Completely at ease with the situation, I slowly push the seat back. Monica turns her head and asks:

"Should I keep going?"

"Yes, you're fine. Don't mind the people."

"Are you sure?" Without responding, I gently push her head next to my crotch, close my eyes, and think. Where am I? Okay, let's back up. What's the last thing I remember? As I try to embark on a retrospective path, Monica is doing too good a job. So I focus on the present. I focus on the now. A sudden resemblance to meditation takes over my mind until I finish. A glorious release runs through my whole body, extending into my fingertips, eroding energy toward the universe.

"Hey, are you in for a wild taste or what?" she asks, a hint of mischief in her voice, a trait I always find kind of funny. It's moments like these that I realize why I'm attracted to her—she's unpredictable and vibrant, but she is also out of her mind.

"Are you nuts? Why would I try my own load?" I answer, almost offended.

"Some men love to," she answers dismissively.

"Yeah, well, that isn't me."
It's been two months since we've been sort of dating—this casual but intense thing we have going—and this is the first time she asks me that, which makes me wonder if she recently had sex with a guy and made

him try his own load. She laughs and slowly reaches for her purse. With delicacy, she pulls out a little pink-cased kit. The kit contains syringes, a cooker, cotton filters, a rubber strap, a lighter, sterile water, a razor blade, and a plastic doggy bag—all the necessary accessories to inject crystal meth. The funny thing is that the plastic bag is to throw everything away nicely in the trash: the feminine touch of a drug addict. It sounds like an overfunded Netflix miniseries. Personally, I'm not a needler, but Monica clearly is.

The fact that she works while high is beyond me. She spends a lot of time in the gym, too, pushing her body to its limits, perhaps trying to outrun her demons or the creeping fatigue that her lifestyle inevitably brings. It's almost an art watching her inject meth; she sticks the needle exactly where the bicep vein pops up, so she has no marks on her arm. Amazing. With both hands, I make the universal finger signal for "fuck off" to my faithful public and start the engine. Eleventh Street in Miami's downtown roams with prostitutes at this hour. The sunlight emphasizes the watermarks on the hood of my 2010 black Tahoe, reminding me why I hate black cars—or navy blue, for that matter. Although they convey a sense of cleanliness, it's absurd how many times they need to be washed. Monica rambles about a waiter not giving proper tips to the busser, but I couldn't care less. As I get home and step onto the elevator, I feel a sudden weight on the back of my head, like melted iron creeping in, not letting me think straight. The hangover is coming sooner than expected, and this is taking forever. I cannot even open my eyes anymore.

"Are you okay?" the old lady riding the elevator asks. I turn with a Kubrickian look, as if I'm going to kill her, then affirm with a gentle nod and my eyes closed. Monica jumps in:

"He's fine; he just partied too much." I cover my forehead with my hand and blast off the elevator as soon as we reach the floor.

I tell Monica to cook some eggs as I blast through a Gatorade with a couple of ibuprofens. I eat voraciously and jump into the shower. Damn, it feels good. I'm healing. Every drop from the showerhead lets me know that everything is going to be okay. It's time to embark on that memory journey. What happened last night? Oh shit—I tried Julio's ketamine. The water streams down my face, and as I close my eyes, last night starts to materialize behind my eyelids.

The memories flood back as clearly as the water hitting my skin. I could hardly walk, as if my feet were submerged in a pair of buckets filled with cement. I felt great, though. Perhaps I was even talking more slowly, but I wouldn't know; I was so deep into the music that time felt slower. It was weird that even though I was having the time of my life at this club, my real life was melting, just like my body. This duality affirmed that we can be in both a good state and a bad state at the same time. I had to understand that it was okay to feel bad, but I wouldn't get into that right then. I just wanted to let go, to let go into the soothing vibes of the music. From his frantic movements, I reckon that my friend was having an entirely different experience. He said that the lights made him feel like a cloud floating above the crowd. Evidently, we were under the influence of different drugs. My slowness came from special K intake. Ketamine is as if your brain decided to hit the reset button but left a few wires unplugged just to see what happens. Technically, it's a dissociative anesthetic—meaning it doesn't just numb you; it turns the volume down on reality itself. But calling it an anesthetic feels almost insulting because it's so much more ambitious than that. Ketamine doesn't just dull the pain; it gives your mind a hall pass to wander the hallways of existence, casually questioning why it signed up for this in the first place. It feels like someone hacked into your brain, flipped the gravity switch, and said, "Let's see what happens if we just float for a while." There's a weightlessness to it, as if your body has the microphone and your soul is backstage, controlling it with broken strings. Time slows to a crawl—or speeds up—or maybe time just decides to call in sick altogether. It's like your thoughts get an all-access pass to a new dimension where nothing makes sense, and yet everything feels oddly poetic. But here's the kicker: despite its techno-spiritual chaos, ketamine somehow carries this weird sense of clarity. You're questioning the nature of existence while simultaneously wondering why your hand feels like it's made of marshmallows—but you've also never been more certain about how much you hate the texture of carpets.

It's therapeutic in the sense that it temporarily disconnects you from all the nonsense you think you have to care about and forces you to just be. On the other hand, MDMA is a stimulant with empathogenic properties, which is a fancy way of saying it turns your emotional dials all the way up to "I love you, man!" You don't just feel good on MDMA—you feel like you've cracked the code to happiness, and it's written in the way someone smiled at you or how the bass in the music seems to sync perfectly with your heartbeat. Your senses don't just sharpen; they throw on rose-colored glasses and start delivering TED Talks about how wonderful the world is. Touch becomes electric, music becomes spiritual, and your thoughts transform into Hallmark cards on speed.

The scene was a classic techno scene. Two big screens displayed random images related to the DJ. Generally, the images convey the vibe the artist wants to portray. I was so confused by watching Mario Tennis images from Nintendo 64; I can't remember why they were displaying them, though. Was DJ Tennis playing? It had become a habit of ours to participate in the techno atmosphere of the city and party a lot, at least on weekends. Two fundamentally good reasons backed our—what most people would call—drug-addict behavior. First, it felt amazing. Second, the best women in Miami—and arguably the world—were in these places. To make my point, the lights started to go out. That slow brightness filling the room seemed to bring a hint of sobriety with it. Soon enough, across the room, I saw a couple of women I was eager to say hello to. Louis said, "Hey, aren't those the Mojave twins?" With a disappointed nod, I concurred. They were almost nice, but we never got to actually meet them. I think one is an alcoholic; I have no idea what she's doing here. I made a slight wave and got no response. My sight bypasses the twins, and I see Monica at the bar. She must have arrived at the club separately; I hadn't noticed her until now. Louis already knows where this is going and says, "I have to work in a couple of hours; let me know how it goes." The water had gone cold. How long had I been standing there? My fingers were pruned, and my mind, still foggy from last night's excesses, was slowly piecing together the fragments. I shut off the shower and reached for a towel. The bathroom mirror revealed bloodshot eyes staring back at me—eyes that had seen too much and felt too little. As I wrap the towel around my waist and dive into bed, my phone buzzes on my nightstand. Damn it, I have a meeting in two hours. Okay, if I sleep for forty-five minutes, I can make it just in time. It's quite a plan. Even though night sometimes overtakes me, I consider myself organized. Forgetful, but organized.

Chapter 2

I can't believe I missed the meeting. My forty-five-minute rest mutated into a six-hour sleep. My phone's screen is a mosaic of missed calls and red-dotted notifications, among them a terse message from the lawyer's office saying that I'm being charged for the no-show. Well, yeah, right. Mr. Eric Goldman is only interested in the meeting because he can potentially get a nice payout from a diamond-trading company. The clock reads 2:17 p.m. Wasn't it just morning? Shit.

My father navigated the shadowy atmosphere of the diamond trade for decades—this profession forces you to operate in vast ethical gray areas, and honestly, I don't have the charm he had to grow relationships in "respected circles." I couldn't care less, actually. There is an art to the diamond trade: maintaining relationships. This is a world where relationships are currency and charm is the primary negotiation tool. Rick Rubin says that anything can be a work of art—it could be a conversation, the solution to a problem, a note to a friend, the arrangement of furniture in a room, a new route home to avoid a traffic jam—or, in this case, managing relationships. My father was an expert at that. He would definitely know what to do in this situation. I imagine he's standing by the window in his favorite jacket, pointing at the contract. I shake my head to focus.

I'm in the dilemma of getting screwed over or being eaten by a world I know nothing about. Diamantina Trading is offering me almost a quarter million dollars for the five percent equity my father held. From basic math and my accountant's evaluation of last year's financial statements of Diamantina, I know I'm getting about fifty cents on the dollar for that deal. Eric just wants to sign because he gets half of the "super" deal he brokered. That money would give me a couple of years of not working as a bartender and not getting too crazy at parties. I would love to receive dividends, but the board wants me out, and that's my dilemma.

As I get out of bed, I head to the kitchen to drink what feels like a gallon of water. I grind some toasted Guatemalan coffee beans, pour them into the coffee machine, and hear the satisfying noise of boiling water navigating the tubes to release a medium-roast aroma. With a satisfied face, I enjoy the kitchen being reasonably clean—I'm sure it was Monica who pitched in. I take my favorite coffee mug—a white mug with black bold letters that read "Ash is our purest form"—and head to the terrace to contemplate North Miami's landscape.

Sporadic palm trees rise among varied vegetation, dominating my view all the way to the horizon, and a baby-blue sky with arrogant white clouds perfectly completes the scene. As I ponder and feel grateful to be alive, Eric calls me again, and before getting a patronizing speech mixed with a whining complaint about the deal falling through, I decide not to answer. I look at my phone, clouded with red notification numbers: a bunch of spam emails that seem to multiply like bunnies by the hour, some iMessages, and one WhatsApp message from some guy:

> "Hi, Ryan, I'm Carlos Echenique, writing on behalf of Hacienda Galeria de Arte in Caracas. It is of great importance that I talk to you in relation to Camila Torres's Resplandor Interior collection."

I definitely don't want to get into any Venezuela problems right now. Plus, what's Resplandor Interior? He must be mistaken. Besides, everyone from my mother's family hates me. Erika, my aunt, is the sole exception—she still checks up on me, despite our not seeing each other in two decades. I wonder how things are over there. I have another message from Devon from hours ago. I pause, trying to recall who Devon is.

"Thanks for the discounts on the shots yesterday. You sure have some cup skills"—referring to my bartending trick of throwing a bottle high in the air, creating a perfect arc around me before catching it in the aluminum mixer. "Wanna come to the yoga sunset party I mentioned yesterday?" she follows up.

Now I know who she is: Devon was one of the most beautiful girls I've seen in a while. In the dim light of the bar, I distinctly remember her—red hair, piercing bluish eyes. She was concerned about her friend's birthday, wanting to buy shots for a group of fifteen. I'm a gentleman but not a pushover. A $400 tab was out of the question, so I gave her my discount. Less tip, but definitely worth getting her attention.

"Count me in," I text back.

"We're meeting at Coral Gables port in half an hour."

 "Hmm.. I'm kinda far. Where is the boat docking?"
"On a little island just next to the 395 bridge."

"I live close by. Maybe I can reach you guys later in my kayak."

"Amazing!! Yes, I'll wait for you."

"See you soon, babe."

Shit, that "babe" sounds weird now that I think about it. And it would be worse if I erased it after she saw it. I have to own it; it's not the end of the world. Also, I have to relax. I still have a couple of hours to get there. Although I haven't thought this through. What exactly is a yoga sunset party going to be like? Will there be alcohol? How am I supposed to be funny without alcohol or drugs? The more I think about the scenario, the more anxiety builds, like steam pressuring a forgotten kettle. I can't go alone.

"Dude, wanna go to a party this afternoon?" I write to Louis.

Okay, I'll be fine if I have support; we can take some drinks, maybe some molly. As I wait for Louis, I have to organize myself. I still have a small headache, so I'll go Anthony Bourdain style: spicy Szechuan food, ibuprofen, Coke, and weed. Although I'll take just one small hit of weed because I don't want paranoia taking over my personality.

"Can't, I'm taking a girl out tonight."

"Who? Send pic."

"Tiffany." (Screenshot of Tinder profile picture attached.)

"She looks like she's had chlamydia at least twice."

"Fuck off."

After texting two other people with no luck, I realize that I can't let this opportunity slide, so I'll embrace this voyage by myself. Time to figure out the worst-case scenario. The most dreaded thing is that she loses interest, which would mean not making an effort to get to know me. That could leave me isolated in a crowd full of strangers. But I always have my failsafe, my wild card with a one-hundred-percent success rate: my parents died in a plane crash fifteen years ago. The drama and nostalgia from that sentence bring automatic attraction—though it has an expiration date if not managed properly. Mismanagement often happens with women I like. Veronica, my only female friend, says I'm a sociopath for using tragedy as a seduction tool. I prefer to think of it as a slightly cynical approach to human connection.

The food arrives—spicy Szechuan chicken, special fried rice, and fried wontons. I crack open an iced Coke to pleasurably wash it down. And that's it; nothing beats this combination. I decide to slightly deviate from Mr. Bourdain's effective hangover cure, substituting the joint for a masturbation session. The endorphin release should make me drowsy enough to have a quick nap, leaving me ready for the party. My timer goes off, and I'm ready. I gather the essentials: black Electric surf sunglasses, cash, ID (in case my body is found in the middle of a beach), a yellow thirty-ounce waterproof bag, Apple corded earphones, bar-stick sunscreen, quick-dry towel, a Hydro Flask water bottle, one gram of molly, a flask with three ounces of Venezuelan rum, and a Travis Mathew golf hat. Last but not least, I get out my dark-blue single-person sock-style kayak—everything I need to make it to a party with complete strangers. A genius move on my part to buy a blue kayak to paddle in an ocean.

I keep the kayak towage kit in front of my parking space, which I assume irritates a lot of the old, fancy retirees living in my building. These guys are everywhere: red cheeks, fat, sixty-something guys wearing tucked-in polo shirts, khaki shorts, long white socks, and New Balance 407s. It's practically a uniform here in the building. Despite many encounters with my neighbors about noise, parties, and "lifestyle choices," they've never complained about my kayak hogging extra parking space. Small victories.

The lobby stands as a monument to a faded style: golden-tubed luggage carts, travertine-marble floors, red leather furniture, and a sky-blue colossal carpet breaking up the space. There's a vibe that just screams Miami in the eighties. Fuck, I love it. I secure the kayak to the truck's roof and drive through the building complex toward the pier. There's nothing particularly exciting about the pier except that it's for private use, only for the building's residents. Still, it's a getaway for my mind. As I walk the wooden plankway with my sky-blue kayak on top of my head, I feel great. The combination of excitement and the invigoration of carrying the kayak transforms my mood completely. Some people call this power posing, others kinesthetic awareness—either way, the nonverbal behavior influences my feeling of power.I slide the kayak into the water, and off I go.

My kayak slices through the choppy water; each stroke is a battle against my hangover, which is almost nonexistent by now. After about a thirty-minute paddle, I reach the 395 bridge. The concrete structure cuts through Miami's landscape like a sharp knife, ninety-degree angles shaping buildings at the end of each entrance. As it towers overhead, long shadows cast over Biscayne Bay. I see several boats not far away, pushing me to cross quickly. To my right, the Miami skyline rises—glass towers reflect the merciless sunlight, looking both pristine and imposing. This city doesn't apologize, much like me. In the distance, I see what appears to be a party boat.

"Hey, I'm ten minutes away," I text Devon.

As I get closer, I get a better look at the vessel. Still no response, great. I realize I've never seen one of these party boats before while sober or during the day. They're remarkably ugly—a white monstrosity where the top and bottom sections don't really seem to fit together. The flybridge seems like an afterthought, like someone stuck a Tupperware container on top of the main deck. No flow or lines, just two completely different boats stuck together. About ten feet away, a couple of girls on the stern make a friendly approach, almost shouting:

> "You wanna join? We have kombucha tea!" they scream.

> "Sure, let's do it," I reply in a matching tone, thinking, These women are gorgeous. If they're half as nice as they are hot, I might actually enjoy myself.

I refuse to shout that I'm Devon's friend like a needy prick. I'll keep it light and cool. I grab one of the hanging ropes and tie it to the cleat. I'm drenched in sweat, so that's probably not good. I take off my Pelagic long-sleeved shirt and go into the water without thinking. Underwater, I hype myself to match the vibe and think, I got this. As I climb aboard, both women eye me in a hawkish, almost seductive way. Good sign—they find me attractive. They both have Stanley cups in hand. Most people think that if you're attractive, everything is done. Newsflash: you only have half your dick in, and if you're not confident, everything can go down the drain in a second and you'll be labeled as "boring." What constitutes "boring" can be subjective, depending on who the juror is, but confidence is universally recognized. When the time comes, you either have it or you don't.

For someone with intrusive thoughts like me, this can sometimes be challenging. So the trick to avoid an anxiety spiral of trying too hard to be funny or interesting is: stay present, don't be an asshole, and offer sincere compliments (one-hundred-percent guaranteed with women). If you get mixed up in confronting or trying too hard, anxiety can come knocking, and you can enter what Mark Manson calls the Feedback Loop from Hell—getting anxious in a situation, identifying that you're anxious, then getting anxious about your anxiety, entering a loop from hell. You don't want that.

After drying off and grabbing a fresh shirt, I approach the women. The blonde to my left has a sun-kissed figure—she extends her arm, with a tan gleaming under the sun, along with what seems like a dozen bracelets that match her brown bathing suit. The silver material accentuates the perfect lines of her torso and lips. Clearly out of my league.

"I'm Chloe, nice to meet you. She's Sofia," Chloe says with a soothing voice.

"Holy shit, you're both beautiful," I reply, trying to include Sofia in the compliment.

"Haha, thank you," Chloe says, shifting her tone to playful skepticism. "So, tell me, do you just jump in on random people's private parties?"

"No, just the ones that invite me to have kombucha tea," I quickly reply without missing a beat. The moment the words leave my mouth, I know I've nailed it. Piece of cake so far. They both laugh, and I follow up with:

"Do you guys know Devon?"

"Yes! Of course, she's upstairs," they say, maintaining a light and friendly tone that keeps my confidence up.

I head upstairs, the deck vibrating with soft ambient house music—it goes with the emotions of the party, a relaxed and mellow atmosphere. Devon spots me from across the deck, and our eyes lock. She has a patterned scarf covering her fiery red hair, making her more striking against the blue water behind her.

"Oh my God, you made it!" she exclaims, genuinely pleased.

"Barely, I'm still kinda hungover from last night."

"Well, you're here, and that's what matters," she says, laughing.

"Yeah, thanks for inviting me." Realizing I'm not giving her much to work with, I look around the deck and, with an expression of curious confusion, gesture with my hands. "So, what exactly is a yoga party? Are you guys drinking?"

"Well, not all parties need alcohol," she says, almost defensively. "But, yes," she adds with a slight smirk. "There's an open bar for beer and smoothies; we don't want people too fucked up before the yoga class." She looks at the waterproof bag in my hand, full of stuff, and says, "I see you came prepared with a bag and everything."

"I didn't know what to expect, so I brought just the essentials for a party. Just in case," I say with a subtle smile.

"Hmmm, love it," she replies with an intrigued, approving face.

"Devon!" a guy screams, cutting through our conversation. He seems like either the owner of the boat or, more likely, the person who rented it. He's the only guy with a flowered robe and a bandana on the boat.

"Hey, I'll be right back—my friend's calling me," Devon says. "But have a smoothie or a drink! The class starts in an hour."

Great, I think to myself. She hasn't introduced me to anyone yet, and exactly what I feared is happening: I'm sober at a party with a bunch of people I don't know. But at least I can assess the situation properly.

The flybridge stretches about fifty feet long. I can't be certain, but it feels like the length of a bowling lane—not huge, but long enough for people to space out. There are maybe thirty people. To my left, four coffee tables with poufs along the railing give a vaguely Moroccan vibe. To my right, nothing but empty space until the bar at the corner where Devon is with the guy who just called her over. I hope he's gay; if not, he looks like a douche. There's an empty pouf just next to me, so I decide to take a breather. I check my phone, and there's a message from Tyler, my boss: "I need you to swap tomorrow's shift for tonight." I consider my options and decide to see how tonight unravels first. The night shift doesn't start until 10:00 p.m., and it's not even sunset.

When I look up, Devon is looking right at me, along with her friend of undefined sexuality. Shit. When women look at you from a distance, they're noticing you. In most cases, if there's already established contact, or even if there isn't, approaching is the logical move—it projects confidence. If you exchange glances and take no action, you come across as introverted or insecure. Easy choice: I decide to walk toward them. I stand and walk across the deck, thinking, What am I doing here? I'm in no mood to socialize. Either way, I think I'll just be here for about half an hour more before making my exit.

"How you doing, buddy? I'm Ryan," I say, opening the conversation with a smirk just short of a smile.

It's fascinating how we use references when approaching strangers—especially men: bro, brother, champ, man, dude, among countless others. I've come to realize that people often use these terms to assert social ground. There's a sort of delicacy in when to use them. Social ground assertion can tilt toward camaraderie or dominance. This is also true when referring to women, yet it's always about establishing confidence. Being a male in foreign territory and clearly attracted to a female, I decided to claim dominance by saying "buddy," with a firm handshake and a friendly face. If you were to place these terms on a scale, "champ" would sit firmly at the dominance end, while "brother" would anchor the camaraderie side.

"How you doing, brother? I'm Matt," he responds.

"So, the party looks nice. Is it the first time you guys have done it?" I address both.

"I know, right? I brought the poufs from my place," Devon interjects enthusiastically. Matt offers no response, which strikes me as odd. Most likely, he's trying to have sex with Devon too, making me the competition rather than a potential friend.

"Yeah, I love them; I like the whole Moroccan vibe," I reply.

"I wanted to bring so much more stuff, but Matt wouldn't let me. I have these gorgeous lamps that would look so cute across the deck."

"Devon, I told you those lamps are too unstable," Matt counters with the weary tone of someone who's had this conversation before. "With the smallest wave, they could fall and break."

"Whatever," Devon says, rolling her eyes dramatically.

"Well, I could really use a beer," I say, putting my hand casually on the bar. "Hey, brother, can you give me the coldest beer you've got?"

"Sure thing, buddy," he replies, reaching for a frosted bottle about to sweat from the temperature contrast. He also deliberately shifts his eyes toward the tip jar.

As a fellow bartender, I always feel compelled to give a good tip. The problem is, I only have three fifty-dollar bills. He's probably earning an hourly wage, and paying a $50 tip for a beer is beyond absurd.

"Shit, buddy, I only have fifties," I confess, leaning slightly. "But I have some molly if you're interested."

"Oh, I'll definitely take you up on that later," he replies, somewhat satisfied.

I notice Devon is dancing with this guy, leaving me no one to talk to. Again. The strategic move would be to get a little buzz going and start talking to randoms, but I'm not really in the mood. I take a rather large sip of the beer and make my way downstairs, slip through the sliding doors of the main deck saloon, and find no familiar faces—not even the blonde goddess I met earlier, whose name I've already forgotten. I just remember the brown bathing suit that elegantly highlighted the curves of her body. I try to look for them, but they're on the beach. It seems like too much hassle just to start a basic "So, what do you do for work?" conversation. I should leave my bag in the kayak. I don't want to carry it around. Reaching the stern, I hear one of the most mellow and sexy voices from behind me.

"Leaving already?"

"Not yet, but soon," I reply, turning my head.

The sun casts her in partial shadow, obscuring her face but outlining a mesmerizing silhouette. My first thought: What's going on with this boat? Are all the women models here?

"How come?" she asks.

She steps out of the glare, revealing subtle freckles cascading from each side of her perfect nose. Her black Ray-Ban Wayfarer sunglasses don't allow me to see her eyes, but I imagine them to be as blue as the water behind her. I realize I've been silent for longer than socially acceptable.

"Are you okay?" she asks.

"Yeah, I'm fine, more than fine. You're spectacular."

"Do you say that to all the women here?" Her tone suggests amusement.

I can tell she's at least ten years older than me, maybe more. I've dated women in their forties before, so age isn't an inherent characteristic that can stop me from hitting on her. Still, I should tread carefully.

"Just the ones that actually are," I reply with deliberate confidence.

"Ha, fair enough," she concedes. "So, are you friends with Matt?"

"No, I'm friends with Devon. Well, I only met her yesterday, so I guess it's a growing relationship," I reply.

"Hmm, I'd say more like a relationship that's at its birth," she counters with precision.

"Okay, debatable. We already had an initial connection and established mutual interest when we met yesterday," I play along.

"Agreed. But in order to grow, you have to establish the foundations of building trust and exchanging positive feelings. Have you discovered any common ground?"

"Shit, well, no. Not yet. We both enjoy drinking shots, I guess. What are you, a psychologist?"

"I am," she confirms with a smile. "I'm also a psychiatrist."

"Oh, so there was no way I was winning that argument. You should've warned me I was talking to a professional."

The conversation flows, but the attraction suddenly plummets like a crashing plane. The worst possible thing happens: as she fixes her amazingly soft brunette hair, the sun reflects off a massive diamond ring that would've blinded me if it weren't for my sunglasses. She's married.

"You're actually holding your own quite well," she laughs. "Have you done therapy?"

"For years. I'm actually changing therapists right now."

"Really, why's that?"

"Creative differences," I say with a half-smile. "Let's say they had their narrative about me, and I had mine."

"That happens more often than you'd think," she replies, studying me with professional interest. "Finding the right therapeutic match can be challenging. If you need anything, let me know." Her tone shifts slightly to a more professional one.

"As in therapy, you mean?"

"Sure, why not?" she replies, giving a casual shrug. I'm thinking that's the worst idea ever, but what the hell, what's the worst that can happen?

"So, what, you already have an analysis of me?"

"Oh no," she laughs slightly. "I tend to unwind at parties; way too much thinking is required to do a proper analysis."

"Alright, what's your number?" I ask, laughing, already pulling out my phone.

"You might want my name," she replies with an amused smile. "It's Elizabeth Silva." As I save her number, she adjusts her ring—just enough for me to notice. "Just to be clear," she continues, "this would be strictly professional. Not whatever you thought when you first saw me."

"Hmm, maybe you're thinking too much of yourself," I say, making her doubt but knowing she's absolutely right.

"Good," she replies with a smirk.

Elizabeth Silva—even her name is hot. I look towards the boat, the strangers, the whole scene. Why am I still even here? Mission accomplished:

1. I kept my word and came to the "yoga party."
2. I met other women.
3. I didn't make a fool of myself. Like in life, you always have to know when to leave a party,

when to leave a conversation, and, most importantly, when to leave a relationship. I'll just quit while I'm ahead.

Chapter 3

My cousin Louis is blathering about another million-dollar business. A guy from his firm allegedly has ties with the Argentine president's wife, and they're helping him launch a meme coin. He's asking if I want to get in. I get distracted by the majestic burger the waiter is putting in front of me. Behold, the double cheeseburger: a two-level prime Angus exotic beauty. Louis keeps talking as I study its satisfying simplicity. The thick patties, enveloped by golden American cheese, almost cover them completely. Below, a vibrant landscape of fresh tomatoes, lettuce, a couple of delicate onion rings, and some pickles peeks out from the front edge. I've considered myself a smashed-burger guy, but when I see works of art like this, my loyalty gets questioned.

"Ryan, are you hearing me?" Louis asks.

"Yes, Jesus, can't you see I have the burger in front of me? I'm starving," I reply, annoyed. I take a bite, buying time to formulate my response. "To be honest, I don't have any money lying around. I've watched these pump-and-dump sketchy projects for years."

"It's not sketchy. It's an opportunity. I'm just trying to help you out. I know you've been struggling to pay the taxes on the apartments," he says in an almost condescending way.

"If you want to help me so bad, why don't you just front the investment yourself? If it's such a sure thing, put money in yourself, we split the profits. That way I'm not risking money I don't have," I say childishly, challenging his confidence in the venture.

"Yeah, right. And you want me to buy you a car too?" he responds, clearly annoyed. "Besides, I'm putting big money in. I think this is a home run."

"Look, bro, I get it," I say, leaning back. "But really, I'm fine now. I was struggling last year because I was partying too much. Now I've got my finances under control—mostly. I'm pulling enough from bartending to cover my expenses. Besides," I pause and add enough crypto knowledge to sound informed, "what if we don't take the money out in time? What do you call that—a rug pull?"

"Oh, the rug pull is coming," Louis says, leaning forward with a smirk on his face. "And I told you I'll get the tip to sell first. That's the game. We know when to get out. Meanwhile, these retail investors..." He shakes his head. "They're idiots. Complete losers. Low-end white-collar workers who think sparing $500 can make fifteen times the return by trying to catch the market," he adds, douchily. His voice drops to a condescending whisper.

"You think most Americanns have access to the financial markets? Do you think they're buying stocks? Think again. Most are just scraping by." He takes a sip of his beer, rather inspired. "The Americann dream has been dead for a couple of decades now, and these 'crypto projects' are their lottery ticket to achieve that dream. But it's bullshit. They won't make money—they'll lose it. All of it. And guys like me are here to collect."

Well, that's a compelling argument—if you're a sociopath. Louis is a couple of years older than me; he works for some Wall Street outfit in New York. A bank, maybe? I'm not quite sure. I've never bothered to remember exactly what he does, just that it involves a suit and preying on other people's financial illiteracy. We've always been this way. When we were kids, Louis was actually a good cousin. Well, he still is. He and his older brother took me to my first strip club in upstate New York when I was sixteen. To this day, I don't know how he pulled that off. That night ended with him pulling me out of the VIP room because I was licking a stripper's asshole. Never do that again, he said. No matter how clean their ass looks. It was good advice, I guess.

"I hear you," I say, "but I just don't have any money for it now." Louis sets his beer down with a gentle tap against the table.

"Alright, but don't say I never tried to help you."

"You can pay for lunch; that's what you can do. Can I eat my cold burger now?" I pick up my burger, and as I take a massive bite of the two-story masterpiece, my phone lights up with an incoming WhatsApp call. Foreign number. No chance I'm answering. The call ends, I glance at my phone, and a green icon pops up with a message:

"Ryan, it's Carlos again, trying to reach you. I'm in Miami. It would be great if we could meet."

"Why aren't you answering? Who is that?" Louis asks. I turn my phone facedown.

"Some guy trying to reach me about my mom's art collection."

"Didn't you want to get a hold of some paintings since forever?" Louis perks up, leaving his financial-predator persona.

"Yeah," I say, my voice catching on the word. "But that fucking family never allowed it." I stare at the plate for a moment, trying to mask the sadness. "I only have a couple of paintings that she made here in Miami, but she was already retired by then." Louis watches me with unexpected attentiveness. He knows talking about my mom's work cracks my usual indifference toward the world.

"Which ones do you have?"

"I only have two small ones resembling a flame. Remember those? I'm sure I've shown them to you. The colors melt and blend with each other, creating a kind of fluid movement. They're fucking amazing," I say, about to get into a deep analysis of the paintings—probably the only thing that makes me feel anything right now.

Another message pops up on the screen. It's my aunt Erika. "Ryan, how you doing, baby? It's been a while since we talked! Look, this guy Carlos has been calling me nonstop about you. Try to reach out to him." Jesus, it's Sunday; this guy is relentless. Louis nods, seizing the distraction of my phone to avoid emotional territory. "Yes, of course I remember. They are indeed amazing," he says with relief. I finish my burger and call Carlos. My hands are steady, but my heart clearly isn't. Is that why I'm avoiding meeting this guy? Do I think about my mom painting, and I get out of place? Fuck no. I've been avoiding it. It's always the same thing: everyone making promises, and I get disappointed in the end.

"Carlos, how you doing? Ryan here," I say in a rather calm tone.

"Ryan, thanks for calling me back," he says. "When's a good time for us to meet?"

"I'm in Wynwood right now. Wanna head over, and we'll have some coffee?"

"Sure, that's perfect. I leave tomorrow," Carlos answers with relief.

I hang up the phone and ask Louis, "Wanna stay for the meeting? I'm sure he's got something interesting to say."

"Can't. I fly back to New York tonight," he answers dismissively. "Alright, I'll get the check and leave you to it." Louis stands up and heads to the register.

I can't figure out if he's disappointed that I'm not investing in his little scam or just disappointed in me. Probably it's me generally. I remember he even offered me a job working for him. Yeah, like I'm going to be his assistant. I'm not exaggerating, but I'd rather grab a 9mm fourth-generation Glock and pull the trigger with the barrel inside my open mouth.

With a rather fraternal hug, I say goodbye to Louis. Despite his views, he's still family. I grab my phone, walk out of the burger joint, and wander around while waiting for Carlos. My mind is torn between Louis's sketchy business proposal and this mysterious Venezuela situation. I make my way through Wynwood's streets, but the heat is infernal. I can almost hear the humidity gathering around me. Sweat starts to slide under my arms. Shit, I have to find air conditioning somehow.To my right, there's a good-looking clothing store, Wynwood Tribal. Well, it doesn't get more Wynwood than this. Racks of clothing with "unique" patterns and textures suggest an individual style rather than a mass-produced trend. I bet Devon's friend got his tribal robe here. Holy shit, Devon. I haven't texted her yet? I must be a special kind of idiot. I just vanished from the party without saying a word. Goddamn it. Well, I've been working two days straight, back-to-back night shifts. I'm exhausted.

"YOUR FASHION + SOCIAL CHANGE" reads in bold white letters with a backdrop of rustic wooden planks. Below the letters, carefully arranged tribal jewelry and handbags try to convey a distinct character. Jesus Christ, where am I, and who decorated this place? It could be worse. Actually, I take it all back, I think, as a gray leather couch appears in front of me. It may be decorated tackily, but it's perfectly thought out, with a rest area for guys. I say guys because no woman would ever sit in a store.

"Is it weird I left the party without saying goodbye?" I text Devon.

Just in front of me, there's a rack holding shorts that look crazy comfortable. I stand up, grab a pair, and hold them up like I'm showing them to the whole store, making an approving face. They're so soft, I think to myself. I check the tag, and the price reads $59.99. Fuck, that's not bad. I'll try on these sixty percent cotton, forty percent polyester shorts made in Bangladesh. My phone vibrates, and I instantly think Devon. But no, it's Carlos.

"Where should we meet? I'm ten minutes away."

"Tiger Coffee, it's on Second Avenue."

"Okay, see you in a bit."

Well, guess what? The shorts look amazing. I'll pay for them and go meet this guy. My hypocrisy has no limits. It took only five seconds to change my perspective about the store.
I arrive first at the coffee shop, sit at a table facing the entrance, and text the guy: "Hey, I'm here, sitting at a table in the corner." I'll wait for him to order coffee. All the tables are to the left of the entrance, so the logical reaction is for him to turn left as he enters. There's just the countertop in front. Five minutes go by, and I'm already immersed in Instagram. The algorithm is mostly showing random Family Guy sketches, coffee techno-day parties, soccer highlights, and endless reels.

A guy enters wearing a green polo and thick-framed glasses and immediately turns his sight to the left. It must be him. I make a hand gesture, make eye contact, and he walks in my direction. As he reaches the table, I stand up and extend my hand for a handshake. I always try to give a handshake standing up as a sign of respect.

"Ryan?" he asks, shaking my hand. "Nice to finally meet you. I'm Carlos Echenique."

"Yes, finally. Nice to meet you, brother," I reply. We both sit down. I start the conversation by mentioning how hot it is, and he concurs. I stand up and say, "I'm getting some coffee. Do you want anything?"

"No, I'm good, thanks," he answers.

"Are you sure? Maybe just water?" I insist.

"Okay, sure, water's fine," he complies.

There's not much of a line, but I have to get the coffee. I hope this guy isn't in a hurry. I check my phone, and there's a message from Devon:

"I think it's weird that you texted two days after, but that's okay." Hmm, what should I reply? The truth, I guess. It's not funny, but it's real.

"Yeah, sorry about that, I worked back-to-back shifts at the bar," I answer sincerely.
No reply.

"Hello, dude, what are you having?" the barista asks me. Shit, I have five people behind me and no idea what to order. I always become the guy I hate: ten minutes in line, and when he gets to the counter, he has no idea what to order. Phone addiction will drive us all mad.

"Alright, just a sec," I reply while he looks at me, almost annoyed.

"Double macchiato with a shot of caramel," I say confidently. "And bottled water."

"Is Smart Water okay?"

"Sure, whatever. The name for the order is Ryan." I open my wallet to grab some cash and see a plastic bag with crystals shining beside the green bills. Ha, I never gave the molly to that bartender; I wonder if he waited long for me.

They give me the drinks rather quickly, and I walk back to the table. Sitting down, I put the drinks on the table, and Carlos gets right to the point.

"Ryan, I was eager to talk to you about your mom's collection. I'm sure you know that over the past few years, your mother's art has been revalued significantly."

"Okay, I didn't know, but go on," I interrupt.

"Her last collection, Resplandor Interior, is valued at 1.2 million dollars," he says, lowering his voice.

"Wait, what exactly is this Resplandor Interior collection? I've never heard of it," I ask with growing interest.

"Yes, Resplandor Interior. It's your mother's last collection. According to your grandmother, you have two pieces that complete the eight-piece collection. She found them in a studio space last year," he explains.

"What studio space? What the hell are you talking about? I thought she made those pieces randomly in Miami," I reply.

"Well, from what it looks like, she started that collection long before she died and finished it in Miami. Your grandmother Carolina sold an apartment studio last year that your mother had, and she found the paintings in a closet."

"That fucking cunt," I answer, indignant.

"I understand your frustration. I've been managing your mother's art for years, and I've come to really appreciate it. I took a couple of classes at the UCV back in the day with her," he says, reminiscing. "Look, I have a friend on the curatorial board at MoMA, and we want to feature your mother's work as a centerpiece for a major nostalgia of Latin American women artists at the end of the year," he says with enthusiasm. "But your grandmother wants to sell the art to a private collector, and she needs your paintings. Without them, the price drops dramatically. You need to talk to Carolina."

Goddamn it. I need a drink. Several, probably. I check my phone in a clearly disturbed manner. Still no response from Devon. I message her again.

"Wanna get a drink today? Maybe we can get something to eat too." I feel Carlos staring at me, still waiting for a response to his remarks. Instantly, I get a message.

"Sure, let's do it."

"Are you free in about an hour?" No response.

"So, what's the plan here?" I ask Carlos, running my hand through my hair. "What am I supposed to do, call my grandmother after twenty years and say, 'Hey, I heard you want the only paintings I have from my dead mother'?" Carlos puts his hand on the table in a placating gesture.

"Ryan, the Galleria in Caracas brokered the meeting with the investor and your grandmother; it's happening next Friday." With a suggestive voice, he continues, "They might get a deal"—he leans back and briefly opens his hands—"or they might not. If you go there and confront her, you might stop the sale."

"And how am I supposed to do that?" I answer with resignation.

"I don't know how to negotiate with her," he says with a shrug.

"And how am I supposed to do that? Do you think I have a million dollars?"

"I don't know, man. I wanted to tell you all this because those paintings are your mother's voice. Her final statement. I would hate for the world to never see them in some millionaire's house."

"But what's your angle here? Galleries make money on sales—private or public."

"Several things. First, I worked with your mother for years, so there's a special bond. Second, my boss isn't giving me a full commission, as he got the client. And third, if the paintings go to MoMA, there's a deal to be made to license your mother's art globally." He glances at his watch, pushes his chair back, and puts his hands on his legs, about to stand up. "Do you even know how your grandmother sold that apartment? Isn't that your inheritance? I have to go, but think about what I'm telling you."

"Yeah, alright, that's actually a good point. Thanks, Carlos."

"Don't sweat it. See you soon," he replies, already assuming I'm going to Venezuela.

As he walks away, I sit there staring at my barely touched macchiato. Carlos is right—how did my grandmother sell that apartment? Was it even hers to sell? And now she's trying to unload my mother's final collection to some rich collector. No way. I don't remember any apartment in my mother's name in Venezuela, but there's clearly a lot I don't know. Still no response from Devon. I wonder why women are like this. She just said she was down to get a drink, and now silence. I pull up my phone again and write to Monica:

"Hey, are you working today?"

"Nope."

"Want to get a bag?"

"You get it, I'll head to your apartment in a few. But only get one."

Great, I need a distraction and to carefully think through my steps.

Chapter 4

Several hours later, I'm sprawled on my leather sofa with a bottled beer in my hand. With a sort of admiration, I hear Monica's take on existentialism. She's wearing my white Uma Thurman T-shirt, featuring the iconic scene from the famous Tarantino movie Kill Bill: Volume 2. She doesn't have the biggest ass, but it's enough for me to appreciate how the shirt outlines her cheeks. She's excited and mostly engaged as she talks about how we're born into this world without a predetermined purpose. She also explains that we're slowly shaped by society's traditions and norms, which ultimately limit our freedom. Okay, maybe she's taking it too far. Her passion is evident, but I'm not entirely convinced.

"So, what, we should live in a world without norms or laws? Where do we draw the line to differentiate ourselves from animals?" I interrupt.

"I'm not suggesting that we kill each other if we feel like it. I'm just saying that without societal constraints, we might take different, bolder approaches," she fires back.

"Give me an example," I reply in a soft, challenging way. At the same time, I look at the glass coffee table with a mirror tray on the edge, next to a cemetery of little plastic bags.

"Okay, think of it this way," she starts. "Society often pushes us toward certain paths, right? Go to school, get a job, get married, have kids—a prewritten script many feel they have to follow." She pauses while I take my credit card to carefully caress a small mountain of white powdered magic. Gently, I move the card up and down the stash.

"Only the bold dare to ignore societal constraints and find different ways of finding meaning—maybe through radical self-expression that society typically discourages," she finishes, proud of her argument.

"I see your point," I acknowledge, "but rules and structures aren't just limitations—they're also frameworks that give us context. Yes, society pressures us to follow certain paths, but without those references, how can we take on alternatives?" I pause thoughtfully. "Let's say that right here, right now, I invite you to play a game."

"Okay," she answers, noticing I've stopped making the lines. "But finish making the lines already."

With a smirk, I say, "Alright, play."

"What do you mean?" she asks, concerned.

"Play the game," I say again.

"What do I have to do?" she asks again.

"That's exactly my point. Without rules, you don't know where to start. You don't know how to win or even how to follow your heart to make the right choice because there's no frame of reference for what to do or what the objective is." I put the tray aside, ignoring her request. "Yes, we're born free, but we're also born without knowing how to exercise that freedom. To make meaningful choices, we need some understanding of possibilities and consequences. The societal frameworks we criticize are also what give us the language to conceive alternatives. And make no mistake, people who love us, tightened by these constraints, want the best for us, but they're guided by the only roadmap they've ever known. They follow the established path, trying with security, I guess, but ultimately for happiness."

"You're conflating structure with meaning," she counters. "The rules don't give us context—they're just artificial limits. The real context is the void we're all suspended in, and the fact that we make up these elaborate social structures just proves how terrified we are of facing that void." I grab the tray and start making the lines again, considering her point.

"Maybe. But I think it's more complicated than just fear. Humans are social creatures—we need something to connect."

The light bulbs in the living room seem to pulse with the beat, brightening and dimming in perfect sync. Okay, focus, Ryan. The television is playing some techno concert set. When did I put this on? The music isn't particularly loud, but it feels like it's stretching like taffy.

Or maybe time is stretching. Jesus, this K is strong, but look at that, I've already finished the lines and didn't even notice. She takes a big-ass line; I just take a bump. Now, with a hint of uncertainty, she replies:

"That's exactly what someone who's never truly broken free would say. You can't know what freedom feels like until you step outside those structures."

"To me, it sounds like an escape more than anything. Do I need to shoot crystal meth to break free?" I ask condescendingly, trying to end the conversation.

"You're a fucking asshole," she says, looking me up and down. "I'm going to the bathroom."

I grab the Marlboro Reds and the lighter from the coffee table and walk toward the terrace. The light beams of the rising sun travel through the glass doors and smash against my body. I slowly put the cigarette in my mouth and feel the smoke entering my body, alleviating my anxiety. Love it. Despite my conflicting feelings about sunrises, I generally like them. They're conflicting because watching a sunrise means I haven't slept, which most certainly affects me the next day. But I love how they look. The first sunrays cross between the palm trees and Miami's buildings. I love this sight. It just bothers me how buildings interrupt the wild atmosphere.

I have to think about what to do about the bomb Carlos dropped on me yesterday. Why's he so interested in me stopping the sale? What's his angle? If the collection is truly valuable, he must stand to gain something besides showing my mother's art abroad. Or not? Maybe he's just a nice guy, and the connection with my mother's art is genuine. I guess I'll find out if this altruism is genuine. Behind me, I hear drawers slamming in the bathroom, then silence. I take another drag, holding the smoke in my lungs. The front door slams with enough force to make the glass door in front of me quiver. So much for another round. Monica's dramatic exit doesn't bother me as much as it should. In fact, there's something oddly peaceful about being alone again. My phone buzzes with an alert: a meeting with Eric today at 2:00 p.m. I don't think I'm making that.

Even if I sleep now, I'll be slow and unconfident. I need to be sharp. I'll push it to tomorrow. But what if Eric can help me? I could leverage the Diamantina drama if he agrees to help. What if the sale of that apartment was illegal? Shouldn't I be the owner of that apartment by inheritance? Then everything inside would be mine, too, including those paintings. Not a bad idea. It's probably a long shot, but it's worth a try.

I send an email apologizing and rescheduling the meeting for tomorrow. I also check my messages; Devon never answered. I guess that's that. Another potential partner's love has evaporated into the Miami breeze. Part of me wonders whether this pattern I've developed will last forever. After a shower, I drag myself to my bedroom and collapse into bed, still wrapped in my towel.

When I wake, I go straight to the bathroom. A familiar splitting headache throws off my balance. The clock reads 4:00 p.m. I'm starving—nothing in my stomach since the burger yesterday. I make myself a ridiculous sandwich and put it in the oven. While I wait for the provolone cheese to melt, I check my phone's notifications. Eric texts:

"9:00 a.m. tomorrow. If you're going to waste my time again, tell me now." Yikes.

"I'll be there," I reply.

I check this week's schedule for shifts at the bar, and I have three days this week. I immediately call my manager to ask for more shifts, but there's no answer. I need something to knock me out tonight, or I'll never get any rest. I'll watch a movie first and then take a couple of sleeping pills and a serotonin supplement for the after-drug blues. Nice combo.

The next morning comes, and I hit the gym to jump-start my system. I make the meeting on time. As I enter the building and the elevator rises, so does my determination. The doors open onto a polished marble floor with Linda, the receptionist, to my right.

I give a barely cordial greeting, as I don't want to engage with the receptionist.

"Linda, how you doing? All good?"

"Hi, Ryan! All good, nice to see you!" she says with a judgmental tone. "Hey, come to the counter. You have two no-shows pending. I need to charge you before you go in with Mr. Goldman." Linda is a woman in her early sixties who, I'm almost certain, hasn't had sex in the past decade. I feel her whole personality is fake. Is it the job? Or does she just hate her life?

"I feel like I'm at the therapist," I answer sarcastically, getting an even more sarcastic attempt at a smile from her. I walk toward her and say, "I'll talk to Eric. I'm sure he can waive them." Two wooden doors behind me swing open, and an artificially optimistic voice calls out:

"Ryan, champ, how you doing?"

"Speaking of the devil," I reply. "Hey, Eric, good, and you?"

"All good. Come in, buddy."

I know Eric sees me as a kid, which I am to him, but at least he cares about me. I don't know if he respects me, but he cares. He helped me maintain both of my parents' apartments—well, for a fat fucking fee, now that I think about it. Eric is a fifty-year-old with the expected look of a lawyer: always suited up—today in light blue with a white shirt and a matching tie. Tanned, big forehead, short combed hair. Former frat boy, no doubt. AirPods in both ears and a Submariner Rolex on his wrist. I, on the other hand, am wearing a black shirt, jeans, black Nike sneakers, and a Garmin watch. I see no need to dress up for a meeting with this guy. Eric gestures to the leather chair across from his glass desk.

"Take a seat." He removes one AirPod but leaves the other in—a power move to suggest I'm only worth half his attention? Who cares?

"So, are we finally going to close this Diamantina deal?" he asks, placing both hands firmly on the desk. "I'm telling you, it's a good deal. These guys will never let you into their company." I lean back in the chair with affected nonchalance.

"Legally, it's my company too. But yeah, I know what you mean." I pause briefly. "Let's do something." He looks at me with a bit more attention. "Ask for three hundred thousand; maybe they'll meet us halfway."

"These guys aren't throwing a penny more," he answers, disappointed.

"I know you want to sign right now, and you've helped a lot over the years," I say confidently, with a reminiscing tone. He shows doubt on his face, sensing I'm building up to something. "Just ask for it. If not, I'll sign anyway. I'm really here because I need your help with something."

"Sure, what've you got?" he answers without hesitating.

"There's a situation developing in Venezuela about my mom's art collection." I lean forward.

"Apparently, my grandmother sold an apartment studio that belonged to my mother last year. She found paintings there—part of a collection worth over a million dollars now." Eric raises both eyebrows.

"And you're just finding out about this now?"

"Yeah, I have to get down there to see what's going on," I say tiredly. "I met with a guy last week from a gallery in Caracas, and he told me a collection from my mom was found in an apartment they sold last year. Now they want to sell the collection, but they need my last two pieces."

"And why does this guy care about your family selling the collection? In fact, shouldn't he be interested in selling? I'm assuming he gets a commission."

"That's the part that doesn't add up. From what I understand, the owner of the gallery brokered the deal, and this guy doesn't get the full commission. Plus, he has a whole spiel about getting my mother's collection into MoMA, which would be amazing, don't get me wrong, but I think it's kind of bullshit," I say, contemplating the situation. "I mean, he says he went to college with my mom and has some sentimental attachment to her art, so I don't think he'd lie about that—it's easily verifiable."

"Well, either way, even though it's fishy, I don't see how he's screwing you. What you want is to obtain the collection, right?" he follows up, genuinely concerned.

"I mean, I bought the whole MoMA story, and whether or not that's realistic, on principle, there's something fundamentally wrong with my mother's art being taken from the world to some private collection where no one will ever appreciate it," I say, reminiscing.

"Look, I feel you. But the negotiation was clear back then: your mother's estate went to your

64

family, and you kept your father's estate here in the US. There may be limited legal recourse after all this time," Eric replies.

"That agreement was made when I was only fifteen—I wasn't even legally capable of giving consent. As the sole heir, there must be something I can do," I say, my voice hardening. "We both know my grandmother exploited my parents' deaths and my youth to take over my mother's assets. I don't want to get into the whole past—just focus on this sale."

"Okay, let's do this: try to get the sale papers for the apartment, and we'll go from there," he says firmly. "We work with a Venezuelan firm in Caracas; they can help us out, but it's going to cost you."

"Alright, close the Diamantina deal," I agree. "Done. I'll get you the papers by the end of the week." I stand up and shake Eric's hand, adding, "Thanks, man. Really."

"You got it, kid," he says with a nod.

Chapter 5

Now I have to get a ticket to Venezuela. It's been twenty years since I was there. Just the thought sends a mix of anxiety and anticipation through me. Where should I stay? Okay, let's see. I could stay with my aunt. Jesus, but I don't know—that might be too much. Should I talk to Cesar? I mean, we're still good friends, I think. I haven't talked to him in months, but the last time he was in Miami, we partied hard. What am I saying? He even passed out one night at my place. Alright, that's the best way; plus, I don't have to pay for a hotel. I get on my laptop and start looking for tickets to Caracas. What's this? Two thousand dollars for a ticket with two layovers—Panama and then Curaçao? This doesn't make sense.

After half an hour of increasingly frustrated searching, I realize there are no direct flights to Venezuela. My best guess is that political tensions have severed most direct routes. It's hard to keep up with what's going on over there. The easiest way is to go through Mexico, so I try to complete the payment on the Conviasa website. This website sucks. Shouldn't the payment process be the easiest part? I want to purchase the goddamn thing. No luck. What do I have to do—hire a travel agent? Jesus, am I in the right decade?

Thanks to Instagram listening to my thoughts, I get a promo for cheap flights to Venezuela from Viajes Marco Polo, obviously a travel agency. I hope it's not a scam. As I write to them, I gauge their engagement: two thousand followers on Instagram, which is terrible, but the like-to-follower ratio is about one percent, suggesting the followers are real. Not many comments, but none are bad—another good sign.

"Hello, looking to fly to Venezuela this week."

While I wait for a response, I check their website. A promotional reel autoplays, showing a blonde woman with blue eyes making a "come here" gesture with her index finger. She must be some kind of model. The website looks like they spent serious money on it. My suspicion of it being a scam is officially over.

"Good day! Exactly which date were you considering?" The phrasing makes me picture a young woman with perfect posture typing each word with deliberate care.

"Any day this week works. I'm traveling from Miami," I reply.

"Perfect, one moment while I check availability."

I stare at the screen, but my mind drifts. The appointment with Elizabeth—Dr. Silva—is in forty minutes. Brickell Medical Arts Building, Suite 708. The address is in my conversation with her. Just enough time to shower and look somewhat presentable. I'm not sure why I care what I look like for a therapy session, but something about Elizabeth makes me want to put in effort. Strange how she quickly offered me an appointment. If she's that good, shouldn't she be booked for months? Maybe she's a terrible therapist. A notification from the travel agency pops up, breaking my train of thought:

"The next available flight is next Thursday, in two days. It would be $1,200 for the round trip." I pause. Should I book it right away? Venezuela, my mother's paintings, confronting my grandmother—it all feels surreal, like a problem from another life. Besides, how much am I going to spend there?

"Okay, that's fine. Do you take credit cards?" I answer, feeling like a businessman but, in reality, just an average bartender on a tight budget for this trip.

"Sure. I'll need your personal information, including your passport and email. I'll send out the payment link there."

Okay, this was fairly easy. I send her the information, then close my laptop. The travel agency has my details, I'm on time for my appointment, everything's in motion. Standing up, I feel briefly dizzy—probably the lingering effects of whatever I took with Monica. I steady myself against the wall and head to the shower. Clean body, clear mind. That's what my last therapist used to say before I fired him for being a patronizing asshole.

I throw on a white linen shirt and dark jeans after my shower, aiming for the sweet spot between "trying too hard" and "complete mess." The midday heat hits as soon as I step into the parking lot, making me grateful for the Tahoe's powerful AC. The GPS leads me to Brickell, almost to the end of it. I expect another tall glass building, but instead, I find myself turning into a sprawling Mediterranean-style complex that looks like a luxury resort that hasn't been properly maintained in years. The building is actually a complex of interconnected two-story buildings arranged around courtyards filled with fountains and plants. Corrosion and watermarks on the sides of some buildings confirm my suspicion of poor maintenance. Terracotta roof tiles and warm cream exterior tones contrast with the wrought-iron balconies, giving a kind of European vibe. A series of arched—some broken—walkways connect the buildings. I make my way to building seven, where a bronze plaque lists the units.

Unit 708 has a rather austere nameplate reading "Elizabeth Silva, MD, PhD." "Dr. Elizabeth Silva" would seem nicer, I think. And what if someone moves? Do they have to change the plaque every time? Who pays for it? I look at my watch, and I'm right on time. The clock reads 2:28 p.m. The unit is immediately to the right as you enter the hallway—the door is closed, and I hear voices inside, suggesting she's with another patient. There's a sofa just outside, so I sit while I wait. A large framed painting on the wall in front of me catches my eye. It's a modern piece showing what appear to be oranges with wings, maybe flames. The more I stare at it, the more I see in it— perhaps a phoenix rising or a person with arms outstretched. It's either portraying agony or ecstasy. Either way, the ambiguity seems deliberate, almost challenging. Is this some kind of psychological test? The door opens, interrupting my thoughts. A middle-aged man, avoiding eye contact, hurries past me.

"Ryan?"

Elizabeth stands in the doorway, looking nothing like the woman I met at the party. Her hair is pulled back, she wears little to no makeup, and her outfit is a conservative charcoal pantsuit. One thing is different: I can see her eyes now—penetrating green eyes surrounded by golden flecks.

"Come in," she says, stepping aside to reveal a dimly lit office.

"You got it, Doc."

As I pass her, I catch her scent—a subtle, fruity cocktail perfume. Was she wearing it at the party? I can't remember. The office surprises me; the space feels meticulously considered. The walls are painted a navy blue that somehow makes the room feel larger. A leather armchair sits at an angle facing the couch, both worn but seemingly intentional. The bookshelves catch my attention because they don't hold standard psychology textbooks but literature: Dostoyevsky, Camus, Borges—serious stuff, most of which I'm not familiar with. A few small artifacts are scattered among them: a small bronze sculpture, some rocks (quartz, my best guess), and a couple of diplomas on the wall. No family photos.

"Please, sit wherever you're comfortable," Elizabeth says, closing the door behind us.

The lock clicks with soft decisiveness. I sink into the couch, surprised by how comfortable it is. Elizabeth takes the leather armchair, crossing her legs with a practiced elegance that reminds me of our encounter on the boat, despite her transformed appearance.

"So," she begins, her voice slightly warmer than her professional attire suggests, "you mentioned at the party that you were changing therapists." With a hint of amusement, she adds, "Something about creative differences?" The question catches me off guard. I expected the usual first-session dialogue—family history, reason for seeking therapy, or insurance paperwork—but she's picking up right where we left off.

"My last therapist was convinced everything circled back to my parents' deaths. Fifteen years later, every decision I made was questionable. Every relationship, every insecurity, every hangover was reduced to grief," I say, watching her reaction.

"Reducing someone to their trauma is another kind of prison," she says with unexpected candor. There's admiration in her expression, like she's genuinely intrigued. She uncrosses her legs and leans slightly forward. "Though, to be fair, your therapist might have been right. It's a very Freudian approach—believing everything stems from childhood trauma."

"It seems to me the easy analysis is pinning everything on my parents' deaths." Elizabeth leans forward slightly.

"I tend to follow Alfred Adler's approach to trauma. Do you know his work?"

"Not really. I only know he's one of the big ones."

She smiles, tucking a strand of hair behind her ear, which I find increasingly sexy despite my efforts to keep this professional. "I don't want to bore you with a lecture, but it's important you understand how I work. Adler believed we're not determined by our past but drawn toward our future. We create meaning through the goals we set. Of course, this event shaped you, absolutely, but it's not the only thing that defines you," she says with surprising warmth. I find myself nodding and admiring her at the same time. There's something refreshing about her approach—intelligent without being condescending, warm without feeling fake.

"So, tell me," she says, her eyes meeting mine, "what actually brought you here today? I'm guessing it wasn't just to debate psychological theory."

"It was more of a lecture than a debate," I say with a hint of sarcasm, then hesitate. "I keep finding myself in relationships that go nowhere, always with women who are damaged or unreachable. I'm thirty and have never been in love—or not really, I think. It's like I'm stuck in this pattern of dating women where there's no future.

"And now I have to go back to Venezuela, and I know tension's coming. I usually just numb myself when I feel fear or stress."

"And by that, you mean what?"

"It's pretty self-explanatory, don't you think? Drugs, women, alcohol."

"By drugs, do you mean needles?"

"What? No. Well, mostly stimulants."

I prefer not to go into details about all the types of drugs I do, but it gets me thinking: why would she say needles? Do I look like I'm shooting up? I guess I must look like shit.
"Let's try something. Tell me about the painting you were looking at outside. It's interesting what people see in it. What did you see?" The abrupt change of subject throws me.

"I don't know. A phoenix, maybe?"

"Suffering or transcendence," she says, echoing thoughts I had earlier. "That's why people debate it. Your interpretation often says more about your current state than the painting itself."

"I knew it was a test," I interrupt enthusiastically.

"You could be caught between pain and possibility, trapped in patterns you recognize but can't seem to break." I shift uncomfortably. Her insight is unsettling but captivating.
"Maybe these patterns are signposts rather than obstacles. Don't you think?"

"I've never thought of it that way," I admit.

"Ponder that," she says. "Our time's almost up, but I think we got off to a good start." She stands with that fluid grace, giving me a glimpse of the person behind the therapist persona. I couldn't be more in awe. "Same time next week?" she asks.

"Yeah, I'll probably still be in Venezuela," I say, remembering my flight. "Could we do a call instead?"

"You got it," she answers with a smile. "Just text me when you're settled." As I leave her office, I realize that for the first time in years, I feel truly seen. It's both terrifying and exhilarating.

Chapter 6

For some reason, I love airports. Maybe it's the sensation of new experiences waiting to unfold or the relief of leaving regular activities of your day-to-day life. Either way, I don't mind the wait. Having no Wi-Fi on the plane forces me to read actual books to kill time. It's not easy when you're addicted to electronics, especially when your brain is wired to constant dopamine from digital stimulation.

I gaze up; in front of me, at least twenty people are seated, waiting outside the gate to board, and everyone is looking at their cell phone. Weird how language evolves in what—ten years? There's something about electronics that makes me wonder. For instance, before looking up, I was immersed in my world with an always-perfect algorithm of trivial reels and even motivational stoic quotes. Quotes reflected in a device that turns the message to an ironic tone: "True happiness is to enjoy the present..." I'm enjoying the present while my attention is one hundred percent captivated by my phone? People don't know the valuable commodity that is attention right now. The biggest companies are fighting for seconds on your screen. Our attention is the currency being traded in plain sight.

For example, according to the *Wall Street Journal*, Amazon sold approximately 218 billion dollars in goods last year, and TikTok made only a little more than one percent of that, around 2.5 billion dollars. Yet, here's where it gets interesting: the average user, meaning me, spends around two hours every day on TikTok and only seven minutes on Amazon.

Guess what's happening? They're trying to be like each other, converging into the same dopamine casino: Amazon with endless video streams and TikTok processing payments that allow you to buy the jacket your favorite influencer wore for three seconds. Where does it end? What will we call things in fifteen years? Because sure as hell it won't be phones. Lenses? If neural interface rumors are true, soon your attention won't just be captured—it'll be harvested in real time. The rich will pay for focus; the poor will rent out their visual cortex as ad space. No more phones, just direct neural interfaces. "Add to cart" in your eyes, with data auctioned to the highest bidder. Companies knowing if your pupils dilate with a political ad and then selling that to the government? Our cell phones will just become fossil reminders of how they were tools that turned into ecosystems controlled by the very few. So much for what I'm doing right now. Who wants to live in that world? "Last call to board for Mexico City," the speaker announces.

Okay, I must be losing it, I think, catching my breath. Great, I'm the last one to board; there'll be no space for the carry-on luggage. It's not all bad. I can see which seats are free, maybe change to a better one just before we take off. The boarding pass scanner beeps approval, and I join the line to board the plane.

Inside the plane, I see all the seats filled. To save a couple hundred bucks, I'm sitting in the back, and still no promises of a better seat. I arrive at 34D; luckily, there's space to put my carry-on luggage and backpack in the compartment. Points for the airline's organization, I guess. I make my way to my seat—window, obviously. I've always been a window-seat person. I used to not understand the concept of aisle-seat people, but I get it now: you're free to walk to the bathroom at any time without awkwardly maneuvering past others. Free mobility to the arising opportunity of a better seat. Either way, I prefer my own little spot where I can put the pillow against the wall and let the sleeping pills do their work. Not the case for this flight, I'm afraid—I forgot them.

Thankfully, the middle seat is free; I hope it stays that way. Minding my own business with a reel of a guy wrongfully taken into custody for resisting arrest on Instagram, the worst thing happens: I exchange glances with a guy walking toward our row.

The lady in the aisle seat stands up as he arrives. Yes, this guy, several years younger than me, just ruined my trip. That's fine. I exchange glances again and raise my eyebrows with a subtle nod—the greeting I'd give any stranger. I return to my marvelous story to see how it unfolds as the perpetrator, wrongly accused by a policewoman in a bad mental state, is at the police station with his lawyer, asking for the chief of police to make a formal complaint.

This gets interrupted by the stare of my seated neighbor. I glance back at him and say nothing, thinking he might just be one of those weird people without social boundaries. A few seconds later, he does it again with a more engaging look.

"Can I help you?" I say in a confrontational, surprised tone.

"Yes, you can. You can turn off your phone; it's too loud," he says, quite offended. "Or put on some headphones."

I think, well, this is the rudest guy I've ever encountered. To his point, my phone is a little loud— I'd guess sixty percent of the volume. Certainly not too loud for the rest of the plane, but maybe a bit loud for the guy next to me. Yet my other neighbor didn't even glance at me.

"I don't have headphones," I reply, a lie coming easily. I do have, though, but why should I accommodate someone with such poor social skills?

"I just think it's rude to have your phone so loud," he fires back.

"Look, I get it, but that's no way to approach people. Hang tight; it's just a couple of minutes before we take off."

He was the most offended guy I've ever seen. And I did have earphones, but that's not the point. If he would've approached me with basic courtesy—"Excuse me, do you think you can lower your phone's volume?" or "Sorry, but that's a little distracting," or pretty much anything with a kind approach—I would've complied.

When the plane takes off, I put on my headphones and listen to a prerecorded podcast—pretty much a "fuck you" sign. Now this unleashes a whole other battle: the armrest we share. According to flight etiquette, he should have that armrest, yet most people don't know that. I wasn't abusive, but I gave him three-quarters of the armrest, giving him a false sense of power. Not enough for him, he tried to get the whole armrest. He was trying so hard that I gave it to him in the middle of the flight. You "won," bro.

I wonder whether I was on the right side of that argument—whether I was right to push back. Should anyone blindly comply with every stranger's request? Are we all angry at the world? No one wants to be a doormat, and people without empathy usually bulldoze through life, getting their way.

From the limited collection of movies offered, I settle on some Netflix original, a desperate choice made in the hope of falling asleep before landing. It has a predictably trendy one-word title, starring some actress from that Paris show I never watched. The high production value is evident from the opening shots, but the plot immediately reveals its lack of substance as it follows a lawyer, specifically a DA, in what's clearly supposed to be New York, though they never specify. The first minutes, depicting the death of his father, show promise, but as it continues, the logic collapses. What twenty-something woman becomes district attorney of a major jurisdiction? The premise borders on cliché: the millionaire dead father left a crazy secret that could ruin the family's life. Lazy writing, executed even more poorly. There's a guy hidden in a basement for thirty years on a twenty-acre property that his millionaire father never bothered to check. Okay. What makes me mad is that movies used to come with reliable expectations—a CBS film meant predictable but competent storytelling. Now we're served garbage packaged as gourmet and expected to praise the flavor. How can this be Netflix's featured selection? And how does it maintain a high rating? Have viewers collectively lost their critical faculties?

"The plane has begun descending; you can now see the coast of La Guaira to your right."

Thank goodness. Unexpected joy washes over me, bringing a strange sense of security despite the decades away. Not much has changed from what I remember. As I look through the window, I see ranchos scattered along the coastal strip, making their way up the hill. These small houses, made of blocks and zinc roofs, surround abandoned industrial structures—skeletal remains of a once-thriving economy. The turquoise waves crash against ports with few people on them.

As we land, my contemplation is interrupted by a woman in front of me who barks into her phone: "Is Molina at the gate entrance? I don't want last month to happen again." After a small pause and escalating volume, she continues, "I understand, but I don't want people inside. We'll talk about that later when the plane has landed—tell Molina to be ready."

The lady is carrying a lot of luggage: her purse, a plastic bag full of duty-free items, and carry-on luggage I don't know how they allowed on the plane. Walking just behind her off the plane, a wall of humid air slaps me across the face. Not only that, but two-story stairs stand at the end of the hall to reach the gate. She stops and analyzes the situation. Before watching her make a scene, my first thought is: Damn, I have to help the pedantic lady.

"Do you need help with your bag?"

"Thanks, you're a sweetheart," she answers. My suspicions were true; she's carrying half the duty-free shop in her bag.

We make it upstairs, and outside the gate, Molina is standing in black tactical gear with the word "Interpol" written on the side of his chest, which confuses me. To my knowledge, there's no official Interpol in Venezuela, so the fact that an armed guard carries that name alarms me. Molina takes her bag and greets her.

"Sra. Alvarez, welcome back." She responds with a dismissive smile and directs her attention to me. "What's your name? Thanks again."

"Ryan," I reply, exaggerating my Venezuelan pronunciation by rolling the "R." It's a completely different name in Spanish. Growing up in Venezuela gave me an indistinguishable Spanish accent.

"Oh, you're beautiful," she says, not in a seductive way but almost as a statement, then quickly looks at her phone. "So, what do you do?"

"I'm a bartender." She wasn't too impressed.

"Not here, I assume," she answers, eyeing my all-black Garmin watch. "My husband is the commander of the ZODI for the central zone; let me know if you want to meet him." She hands me a business card with her name and what I assume is the ZODI logo: "Operational Zone of Integral Defense." This is the first time I've heard of this. Okay, there must be a hundred police or military institutions in Venezuela. And why would he want me to meet him? Is this a sexual thing?

"Gracias, que bella," I answer calmly, accepting the card. She might know a judge or something.

The immigration line snakes through the terminal, a disorganized mass of returning Venezuelans. Officials in glass booths process passports at a slow pace. The clearly broken air conditioning allows sweat to form across my eyebrows. Ms. Alvarez accelerates her pace, dismissing me. Each to their own at immigration. Molina follows her, not even acknowledging me. Kind of a prick.

"You land yet?"

"I'm in the immigration line. It's brutal."

"Let me know when you get through; I sent a guy for you."

"Okay."

The elongated flags of Venezuela hanging from the ceiling are more than noticeable. Pictures of the president, Nicolás Maduro, are everywhere—pretty much the same as before, just with Maduro instead of Chávez. Immigration takes longer than expected. When I get to the officer, he stares at my passport with suspicion, flipping through it repeatedly. The officer, a young, skinny guy, says, "This passport expired three years ago." I hand him my American one, thinking it's a bad idea.

"Here's my other passport. I'm going to renew my Venezuelan one."

He looks me up and down, not even glancing at the American passport. "That one won't work here. If you're Venezuelan, you have to enter with your Venezuelan passport. I recommend you renew it; otherwise, you won't be able to leave the country," he says, stamping it.

Beyond immigration, the baggage claim area buzzes with a different kind of tension. Armed guards patrol between carousels while passengers cluster around, eyes darting between their luggage and the exits. With only carry-on luggage and a backpack, customs is surprisingly quick. The dogs don't even glance at me. Thank goodness I remembered to wash all my credit cards. My phone buzzes again.

"You through yet? My guy is at the main exit in a white Toyota. His name is Ricardo."

"Heading out now."

I see Ricardo standing outside a fairly new white Toyota Corolla. He puts my bags in the trunk, and off we go. Afternoon is setting in La Guaira, and it doesn't seem that abandoned. The highway up to Caracas feels the same, cutting right through the middle of mountains with scattered ranchos. Once-unlit tunnels are now illuminated—a minimal effort to spruce up the streets. I really don't feel like talking to Ricardo, and I'm not a huge fan of small talk.

"Good thing there isn't traffic."

"You're in luck. There was massive traffic going down."

As we pass through the last tunnel, we instantly enter Caracas. The highway provides two options: left and right, east and west, low-class and high-class, urbanizations and slums. The imaginary border isn't drawn here, though, as we're still in the west. But it does remind me of the polarization that exists. Many theories exist about who surfaced this polarization, yet the point is that it exists—a city that's become stereotypic in its nature, answering to a social hierarchy in constant change. Or at least that's what I've heard. It makes me wonder where Ricardo stands.

"Where are you from, Ricardo?"

"La Pastora." First time I've heard of the zone.

"And how are things over there?"

"I mean, I'm doing okay with Leo, but a lot of people are struggling."

"Is there lot of insecurity?"

"Not really; that's gone way down. It's the inflation that's eating us all. My cousin is only having one meal a day."

"I can imagine," I reply. But obviously, I don't. I actually have no idea what he or his family goes through or even how he lives. Without getting too involved, I look out the window. The Francisco Fajardo Highway cuts through the city from end to end, this part a two-story plankway. It hasn't changed infrastructurally. It does have more ugly art, though. Heading west, advertising signs increase until they're all you see—on posts and atop mostly old buildings, the newest of which was built thirty years ago. Yeah, this is definitely the border. I didn't remember it like this.

"There are a lot of big buildings in Las Mercedes. I didn't remember it like this."

"Yeah, that's where we're going. Lots of new buildings."

Shining lights from different buildings: one looks like a giant illuminated grid; another modern one has defined lines of light running vertically along the façade, maybe highlighting the edges or some architectural feature. There's definitely a vibe going on here, a changed identity. Most towers have a corporate look with modern structures and restaurants in their lobbies. Gas stations are full, and a KFC looks like it opened half an hour ago. There are at least fifty cars in line for the drive-through. Are they giving away food? Crossing the neighborhood horizontally, at the end of the street, there's a brand-new Ferrari dealership.

"Are we here?"

"Yes, just here to the left."

He drops me at the lobby, which has nothing to envy a Brickell building made this year: a two-story lobby with white floors and white furniture. I pass the reception, which already has my information, and get out on the thirty-fourth floor. I hear music at the end of the hall. It's kind of loud at 7:00 p.m. I get closer and, of course, it's Leo's apartment. No answer when I knock, so I just open the door.

"Holy shit!"

Chapter 7

I slap my face twice under the cold water flowing from the bathroom sink. The polished cement surfaces give a raw, industrial feel—a designer's manifesto of elegance. Each slap brings flashes of last night into focus. Were there little people last night? Three hard knocks on the door bring me back. "Dude, you gotta see this chick!" Leo screams.

I put on my sunglasses and walk outside. Still piecing together fragments of last night, the sun assaults me instantly. Its rays illuminate the rooftop pool, casting diamond-like reflections across the water. Leo rambles about the two women at the panoramic pool. I slowly pull out a cigarette, nodding as if interested. I have a 180-degree view of Caracas. The Ávila, guarding the whole city, is beautiful. I forgot how powerful that mountain is. The waiter catches my eye and signals about two more margaritas. The clock reads 11:00 a.m., and I've lost count of how many "breakfast" margaritas I've had.

"Leo, sit down. I gotta talk to you," I say firmly. "Thanks for last night, really, but I only have a week here, and I have a bunch of shit to do."

"Sure, brother, tell me," he answers, disappointed that we're not talking to girls.

"I need to find the papers for an apartment in Los Palos Grandes."

"What do you mean?"

"My grandmother convinced my aunt to sell an apartment she jointly owned with my mother. I need to find the sale document to see if it was entirely legal."

"And why don't you ask her?"

"I did. She deflected, claimed my grandmother handled the operation, and she just signed. Approaching my grandmother directly isn't an option. We haven't spoken in decades," I say calmly. "That silence isn't accidental."

"Right, right—that whole inheritance mess." Leo nods. "Listen, if you have the basics, like your aunt's ID, it shouldn't be a problem to find that document. Unlike the States, systems here are complicated by design, but everything's solved with money. It should be in the public registry of the municipio, maybe the central one in Chacao. I have a gestor who moves smoothly through public registries. It shouldn't cost more than a hundred bucks."

"Perfect," I say calmly. "That's it?"

"The process is straightforward but corrupt. This guy needs to bribe someone inside the registry to find the document, then make a certified copy. That's it. You'll cover the cost of the copy, but that's minimal."

"Sweet. Alright, let's get in the pool," I say with a smile.
"Last night was fucking nuts, right?" Leo says.

"Dude, I keep remembering shit. Wasn't there a little people dressed as dwarfs?" Leo erupts in laughter, almost choking on his drink.

"You're just now remembering? That was Jorge—there's a whole service where you can hire little people by the hour. He walked around all night with silver platters of tusi. This city's a playground if you've got money. What do you want from me? I haven't slept in three days. Plus, women go crazy for that pink powder. I've had threesomes just for having ten grams of tusi," Leo says proudly.

"How much is a gram?"

"Top-notch? Ninety dollars. That'll make you fly," Leo says, passing me by and making eye contact with the girl behind me.

Okay, in Miami, it's at least a hundred fifty dollars. I extend my arms while I ponder Caracas's passage and take in its contradictions. I love the view. Well, who wouldn't, right? Tusi's not that different from ketamine, though. Its original name is 2C-B, yet many people call it pink cocaine. I don't know the exact contents, but it must contain ketamine and some MDMA, of that I'm sure. Its dissociative features, combined with euphoric stages, create this perfect balance of detachment and pleasure. I don't know who came up with the concept of reinventing cocaine, but they're a genius—a marketing genius. They—or let's not assume gender in the drug innovation space— repackaged substances people were already addicted to, added food coloring, and created a new market segment. And now it's everywhere—from high-end parties in Cartagena to all-night clubs in Madrid and Miami. All for what? A mix of the same shit we've been taking for years. I see Leo getting out of the pool.

"Call the gestor."

"It's Saturday."

"Shit, text him. That way, he knows I'm calling him on Monday."

The sun beats down relentlessly as we lounge by the pool, but I'm exhausted. The day blurs into a haze of margaritas, conversations with strangers, and Leo's endless parade of connections.

"I need to crash," I finally tell Leo. The Las Mercedes skyline seems to tilt slightly as I gather my things.

"Seriously?" Leo ponders, looking at his watch. "Yeah, I probably should sleep too."

"Do you have something to knock me out?"

"Sure, in my bathroom, in the medicine cabinet. I'll be down in a bit; the door's unlocked."

Inside the apartment, I navigate through the aftermath of last night's party. I don't even try to make sense of the remnants. My gaze focuses on Leo's corner sculpture: a bright-red oversized grenade portraying chaos with a deliberate layering of texts and drawings. It's on a white podium in the corner, its reflection bouncing against the podium's window. Words and phrases are scattered around, some partially obscured, like "NEVER 50" in white letters outlined in black and "WHATEVER I EVER WANT" written in black marker on a white patch. Maybe it's a reflection of him.

Leo's duplex is straight out of a luxury real estate magazine, with nothing to envy compared to a Miami apartment. I make my way upstairs to his room to grab the pills that'll knock me out until tomorrow. From the second floor, I can see the clash between pristine design and the magnificent chaos we left last night. The main level is divided by a large wooden breakfast counter, eliminating the need for a dining table. On one side, below me, sits a modern kitchen. On the other side, where the mess is concentrated, there's a living room with a comfortable couch surrounded by carefully curated art. I grab what looks like Ambien, pop two, and go downstairs to the second bedroom. The white linen sheets call me like sirens in the ocean.

The pills do their job—I sleep through the rest of the day and most of the night. When I wake, my phone shows three missed calls from Erika. Right. Coffee. The meeting I've been dreading since I landed. An hour later, I finally meet my aunt Erika at the café.

The place is amazing. The ceiling features a wooden pergola structure with hanging plants in woven baskets, giving it a slightly tropical feel. Various light fixtures, including pendant lights with woven shades and other hanging lamps, provide soft illumination. Several people are behind the bar, seemingly staff members. The waitress approaches:

"Table for two?"

"Yes, but I'm meeting someone. I don't know if she's arrived." I scan the place, and toward the end, I see her raising her hand. I walk toward her, and behind the table, two white columns gracefully support the overhead structure. She stands up with genuine emotion.

"Ryan! Oh my God, baby, it's been so long! I can't believe you didn't come sooner. You know I would've visited if my visa hadn't been revoked."

My aunt talks a lot—always has. She lives in her own world: a bubble of privilege cushioned from reality by family money and a carefully curated worldview. To her, consequences are things that happen to other people. She never worked a single day in her life. Once, at her visa renewal appointment, she lied about the six months she spent in the U.S., and they canceled her visa.

"I know. It's great to see you."

"I'm so glad you came. You have to help your grandmother with all the sales! It's amazing that your mother's work has gotten so far."

"Yeah, I wanted to talk to you about that. I'm not giving away my last two paintings. Those are the only ones I have of my mom," I say in a subtle but serious tone. She instantly changes her expression.

"What do you mean? Really? I have several paintings of hers."

"I can imagine, and I didn't come for trouble, but I haven't talked to Carolina since my parents died. You must know she hates me, right?" I say, waiting for an obvious concurrence from her.

"Yes, I know you guys have had a rough patch, but that's normal." She actually believes her words.

"Fifteen years isn't normal. I've never asked for anything from you guys. My mother had what, over a hundred paintings? Do you really think it's fair that I give away the only two I have?" My words seem to bring her to reality.

"You're right; that's not fair. I'm really sorry you're not part of our family, but that's on you too."

"I'm not here to play the blame game. If you want to compare the reasoning of a teenager who just lost his parents with a whole family of grown-ups, that's fine. I've made my peace with the fact that I only have two aunts as family and a couple of shady cousins. When my other grandparents were alive, I felt loved. They were there when I needed them, and that's enough for me." Erika looks at the floor, almost speechless.

"I guess I never truly knew how you felt." It isn't that hard to imagine how a fifteen-year-old would feel with his parents dying and half his family blaming him for it. But of course, I won't highlight her lack of perception.

"It's fine, really. All this happened a long time ago. I do need your help, though."

"What do you need?"

"I need the sale document for that apartment where the collection was found."

"I don't have that, baby. You have to talk to your grandmother."

"Okay, but you can provide information about the sale: a copy of your ID, where you signed the sale, the address of the apartment."

"Of course. Okay."

"You do understand I have to fight for what's mine, right?"

"I won't get in the middle of it. Do whatever feels right in your heart. If it's meant for you, the universe will show you the way."

I agree with her just to get the information I need. Honestly, I don't know how a person can live thinking like that. "The universe will help you"? Right. If I spend the week with Leo doing lines, will the universe magically help me then? Of course not. Results depend on action, not cosmic alignment. The coffee has gone cold, matching the temperature of our conversation. We drift into ordinary topics—her kids' school, her husband's business ventures, the tennis lessons at their country club. With the conversation in safer territory, she invites me to meet her husband and kids next week. That meeting's probably not happening. She's already planning dinner parties and family reconciliations in her head. But some bridges stay burned, and maybe they should.

Chapter 8

"How is your trip going?" Elizabeth asks over the phone.

"It's been productive so far. I saw my aunt for the first time in years."

"And how did that feel, seeing her after so long?"

"Surreal. She lives in this bubble with no accountability or consequences." I pause, catching myself. "I sound bitter, don't I?"

"You sound angry," Elizabeth observes. "What about Monica? You mentioned last time there might be a pattern with the women in your life." The shift in topic catches me off guard.

"Monica? She's complicated. We had this intense thing, but I blew it with a smart-ass comment. She stormed out of my apartment, and we haven't talked since."

"Why don't you talk to her?"

"I don't know. We have some connection, but she's not looking for anything serious."

"And you are?" Elizabeth asks, her tone suggesting she's caught something in my response.

"I think so." The words surprise even me. "Though it's definitely easier when things stay surface-level. With Monica, everything is intense—the highs, the conversations, the sex. But then morning comes, and we're just two people trying to avoid the crash. Maybe that's why I made that comment about her using." Elizabeth watches me carefully through the screen.

"It sounds like caring about someone feels more dangerous than the drugs."

"Maybe."

I let her words sink in, studying her. There's something about Elizabeth's directness that makes Monica's philosophical ramblings feel hollow in comparison. Even through video, she has this presence—the way she holds my gaze, how she sees through my deflections. The sessions feel oddly intimate. Dangerous territory.

"You know what's actually dangerous? Going back to face my grandmother."

"Ah," Elizabeth says, a slight smile playing on her lips. "I was wondering when we'd get to that."
"That obvious, huh?"

"You've been playing with your watch since we started talking about Monica. That usually happens when you're avoiding something bigger." I lean back in my chair, impressed and slightly unnerved by her observation. "Treating addicts has made you sharp, Doc."

"Deflecting again," she notes, but there's warmth in her voice. "Tell me about your grandmother."

"She's trying to sell my mother's last collection, found in some apartment I didn't even know existed." I run my hand through my hair.

"Fifteen years of not speaking to me, and now she needs my paintings to complete the set."

"What bothers you more—that she's selling the collection or that she's reaching out now?"

"She's not even reaching out. The gallery with the collection did."

"That seems to bother you even more."

"Of course it does. She couldn't even face me herself." I clench my jaw, feeling the anger rise. "These paintings could be at MoMA, you know. But my grandmother just wants to sell them to the highest bidder."

"Have you thought about what you'll say when you see her?"

"I keep rehearsing it in my head, but fifteen years of silence is a lot to unpack. I'll go straight to the point. Why waste time unraveling feelings?"

"Because those feelings will be in the room whether you address them or not," Elizabeth says carefully. "You're approaching this like a business transaction, but we both know it's more than that."

"What's the alternative? Pour my heart out to someone who couldn't even call me herself?"

"The alternative is being prepared for what this confrontation might stir up." She pauses, studying my reaction. "You can go in focused on the paintings, Ryan, but you'll still be sitting across from the woman who blamed you for your parents' deaths."

I get a message from the gestor saying he's downstairs. I end the session. Elizabeth's words about my grandmother echo in my head as I make my way down to meet him. The gestor is exactly what I expected—a guy in his sixties with a worn pink shirt and khaki pants. I can't make out the brand of the car he pulls up in, but it matches his style. I give him the info my aunt gave me and the money—a crisp hundred-dollar bill.

"Okay, I'll have this by next week."

"What? No. I'm not here next week. I need it by tomorrow."

"Look, tomorrow's impossible. Give me three days at least."

"Okay." I'm wondering if this guy will come through at all.

I get in a taxi and head to Hacienda Gallery to talk to Carlos. The thirty-minute ride through Caracas is a masterclass in controlled chaos. A guy on a motorcycle weaves through traffic, going the wrong way on the highway, while the taxi driver barely blinks. "Normal," he says, shaking his head with disappointment. "Yesterday, I saw a car with its back wheel missing. The guy was driving along like it was nothing, with the whole rear axle resting on a beer case."

"What do you mean?"

"I mean the back left wheel hub was resting on a plastic beer case. The case slid along the street, grinding away as a substitute wheel."

Welcome to Caracas, where traffic laws are more like suggestions and survival depends on your ability to dodge random obstacles and other drivers. A street vendor somehow manages to sell coffee to cars stopped at a red light, balancing a tray of cups with the skill of a circus performer. I've been in Miami too long—I'd forgotten how this city operates on its own peculiar logic.

The gallery sits in an old colonial house with white walls and a terracotta roof. There's a nice covered porch area supported by sturdy columns, inviting you to sit and chill. The front of the property has a stone wall partially covered in ivy, adding a touch of rustic elegance. A neat patch of green lawn stretches out in front, making the place feel welcoming. Inside, the colonial charm gives way to stark white exhibition spaces and track lighting. Carlos is waiting in what looks like his office, a small room cluttered with art catalogs and framed exhibition posters.

"Your grandmother's meeting the collector this week," he says without preamble. "They're finalizing the price."

"Hello to you too. Yes, I know I'm talking to her this week." I think this guy's rude; we've only met once. Ignoring my comment, he offers me coffee, which I accept. "Look, I get it. If I don't convince her, there isn't much I can do."

He stands up and asks me to follow him. Carlos leads me through the gallery's main space, past walls hung with contemporary Venezuelan artists whose names I probably should know but don't. At the far end of the gallery, in a space that feels designed for impact, hangs a massive photograph of my mother. She's in her studio, surrounded by the very paintings my grandmother wants to sell. The image must be from the early 2000s—she looks exactly as I remember her, down to the paint-splattered overalls and the way she held her brushes like weapons. The photograph hits me like a punch to the throat. I haven't seen her face in so long and haven't allowed myself to look at pictures. But here she is, larger than life, staring down at me with that intense focus I used to both love and fear.

"Ryan, your mother's work means a lot to us here. It'd be a shame to see it go. Look at this." He grabs one painting from Resplandor Interior and carefully turns it. "Three of twelve," it reads in the bottom left corner. "This is how we know two are missing."

"They're not missing; they're mine."

"You know what I mean."

I find it hard to pin down this guy's intentions. He's right about one thing, though: it'd be amazing to see my mother's work at MoMA. I'd better text Leo to see what he's up to. He answers immediately.

"I'm at El Aranjuez in Las Mercedes. Come have lunch."

"On my way."

The taxi weaves through Caracas traffic, but my mind is elsewhere. Elizabeth's words echo in my head—about how fifteen years of silence will be sitting at that table with us. That might get too intense. Erika should be there as a mediator. She won't intervene much, but she can serve as a buffer if things get too crazy. What about the apartment? Best-case scenario, she sold it illegally. I can offer not to press charges if she leaves me the collection, and if she's still reluctant, I'll offer her my apartment in Aventura. It's fully paid by now. I pull out my phone and start making notes, trying to organize my leverage points. The car swerves to avoid a motorcycle, jolting me back to the moment.

"We're here."

"Yeah, thanks, buddy."

The valet greets me like he knows me. I enter the restaurant, a place I haven't been to since I was a kid. The space has a rustic, warm feel with dark wooden ceilings. Stone walls adorned with old Spanish framed flyers of flamenco and dishes give way to the bar. At the back, a large saloon with several tables set with white tablecloths and sturdy wooden chairs with leather seats. There's a big round table in the middle, and Leo's raising his hand—he's with three other guys. I sit down, and the first thing I see is a twelve-year-old scotch bottle on the table. He calls for the waiter to pour me a glass. Curiously, four other tables have scotch bottles too. It's 1:00 p.m. on a Monday.

The scene strikes me as perfectly Venezuelan—businessmen drinking scotch at lunch, making deals that'd be illegal anywhere else. My father used to come to this place a lot. Same energy, different decade. The waiter appears with my glass, and Leo introduces me to his companions, none of whom say what they do for work.

"Ryan here's from Miami," Leo announces, as if that explains everything about me. The men nod appreciatively, probably assuming I'm loaded. The scotch burns smoothly going down, and I realize I haven't eaten anything today.

"Have you guys eaten? I'm starving."

"Not yet. Sure, let's get some food."

The conversation turns to critiquing Venezuela's idiosyncrasies. In a sort of game, they compete to name the craziest name. What started as a tradition in low-income neighborhoods has evolved into something more complex. Combining the names of parents and grandparents creates a new, original name for the newborn. These names test the limits of the absurd and go beyond, because sometimes it's not a mix of names but a misspelled famous character. They throw around a lot of names—"Yeimes Bon Perez," "Efrofiendlyns"—but the winner is "Yukzelygeman." Beyond the obvious humor and borderline classism, there's a clear detriment in Venezuelan culture to ruining a kid's life because parents want an "original" name. They want to succeed at a game that apparently many people play, but there are no real winners, only losers. The food finally arrives, and the meat looks amazing, with grill marks on each side, served on a wooden rectangular plate. Like many meat joints in Caracas and the interior of the country, they serve it on these wooden rectangular plates—a tradition whose origin I don't know. I grab the hot sauce and mix it with the guasacaca. The combination is perfect. Guasacaca, a flavorful, cilantro-based sauce with avocado, just tastes amazing.

As lunch winds down, the conversation drifts into political and financial schemes I'd rather not know about. I make my excuses to leave. I have to unpack everything that's happened today.

Chapter 9

I don't know how long I stare at Monica's contact on my phone, but the situation still confuses me. Why would she get so mad? Sure, mocking her drug use was a dick move, but we've said worse to each other before. Our whole "no-strings-attached" thing was supposed to be simple: good sex, decent conversation, and a mutual understanding that neither of us wanted more. Lately, there's this nagging feeling that maybe we both want more but are too scared to admit it. The thought of something real with Monica is terrifying—she's as unstable as I am.

My mind drifts to Elizabeth—Dr. Silva—and our sessions. She represents everything Monica isn't: stable, grounded, professional. The kind of woman who could help me get my shit together instead of diving deeper into chaos. But that's why it could never work. She's married, my therapist, and out of my league. Still, I can't help but imagine what a relationship with her would be like.

"Hey, I've been thinking about you lately."

I hit send before I can stop myself. The message hangs there, three gray dots appearing and disappearing as Monica types and deletes her response.

"About what?"

"About us," I type, then delete. Too dramatic. "About that night," I try again. Delete. Finally, I settle on: "About what happened last time we saw each other. I shouldn't have said that."

"Don't worry about it; we were both high."

"I'm in Venezuela. See you when I'm back?"

"Sure."

One word. Maybe that's all this deserves—a casual acknowledgment of our next reunion. No promises, no expectations. It's kind of surprising she didn't show interest in my trip. Then again, I didn't want to explain it by text anyway. Coincidentally, I get a text from the gestor. Found a document. I need another day for the certified copy. "Can you send me a picture of the complete document?"

Finally, some good news. The picture is all I need. As I review the document, it seems my grandmother has legal guardianship over me, or as it says, Tutela Legal. The tutela was justified by my "trauma" from losing my parents. I forward the document to Eric. "Please call me after you read this." Simultaneously, I write to my aunt. "Hey, tía, bendición. I need to talk to my grandmother. Can the three of us have coffee?"

I pace around Leo's apartment while waiting for Erika's response. The legal document feels like a loaded gun, but I'm not sure where to point it yet. From the balcony, I see the Ávila mountain changing colors as afternoon approaches.

"Buddy, how's it going?" Eric calls.

"I'm in this mess. Tell me what we can do."

"The sale is completely legal. After your parents' deaths, your grandmother motioned to the LOPNNA for a 'Medida Preventiva Protección,' giving her legal guardianship over you. Where it gets tricky is that when you turned eighteen, she maintained this guardianship through an 'Interdiction Sentence' from a judge. This judicial decision declares an adult legally incapacitated to manage their own affairs due to alleged psychological trauma. This sentence, though obtained with proper medical evaluation, is still a valid court order until challenged. The good news is that to maintain proper legal oversight of her ward—meaning you—she must have documented regular interactions with you for the last fifteen years, and there's no way she can prove that. I must tell you, if you wish to sue, it's neither quick nor cheap."

"How much are we talking about?" I ask, already knowing I can't afford a lengthy legal battle.

"I wouldn't even know, Ryan. For starters, I can't do it, but I can refer you to people who can." Eric pauses. "Look, you have leverage here. Maybe use this information to negotiate rather than litigate?"

"That's what I'm thinking."

"Let me know how it goes. By the way, the Diamantina deal is done. I'll send you the papers later this week."

"Great, thanks."

"Your grandmother agrees to meet tomorrow at four. The Country Club."

Weird location to pick. Why would she want to discuss this in front of people she knows? I text back a quick confirmation, my mind already strategizing. I don't need to sue her—I just need her to know I could.

The rest of the day passes in a blur of preparation and anxiety. Leo offers to come with me, but this is something I need to handle alone. I rehearse different approaches in my head—should I lead with the legal angle or try for reconciliation first?

Morning bleeds into afternoon, and before I know it, I'm in a taxi heading to the meeting. The Country Club isn't just a club—it's the most expensive and renowned one in the city. The neighborhood stands as a testament to old-money Caracas: a mix of Mediterranean mansions and modern glass houses. Quiet streets lined with massive trees provide shade for joggers and their personal trainers. Security booths dot every corner, guards in pressed uniforms checking IDs and waving through luxury cars. Even during the country's worst times, the Country Club and many neighborhoods maintained their bubble of privilege.

The club itself sits like a crown jewel—a sprawling Spanish colonial building where Caracas's elite have orchestrated business deals and arranged marriages for nearly a century. Of course she'd choose this place, I realize as I enter—it's her natural habitat, where she can ensure the confrontation stays civil under the watchful eyes of her social circle.

I make my way to the restaurant by the pool, where Erika spots me first. She rises with nervous energy. My grandmother remains seated, her silver hair perfectly coiffed, her posture still regal. She doesn't stand. Of course she doesn't.

"Ryan," she says, my name sounding distasteful in her mouth. "You look healthy. How are you?"

"Yeah, okay, let's cut the pleasantries," I say, taking my seat. "We both know why I'm here."

"Do we?" She signals a waiter. "I thought perhaps after fifteen years, you might want to see your grandmother."
"I know you want my paintings, but that's not going to happen. In good faith, I want to buy the Resplandor collection from you."

"That's worth over a million dollars, Ryan."

"I know, and I don't have that. I do have an apartment in Coral Gables, free of debt. It's easily worth four hundred thousand dollars. That's all I've got."

"I wish I could, Ryan, I really do. But the collection needs to stay together." I glance at Erika, who sits there stirring her tea endlessly, eyes fixed on the ripples in her cup—present but absent.

"You know what's happening here is wrong," I say to Erika.

"This doesn't concern Erika," my grandmother cuts in sharply.

"No, it concerns everyone who sat quietly while you manipulated the system," I say, keeping my eyes on my aunt. "How many documents did you sign, Erika? How many times did you look the other way? I have the sale document for the apartment where the collection was found. You have legal guardianship over me? Are you fucking nuts, claiming I'm not mentally well enough to make my own decisions?"

"That was done for your own good," she says, not even fazed that I know about it. Erika, on the other hand, is startled, just finding out about this.

"So, you want to go to court?" I ask, surprised.

"Do what you have to do, Ryan."

"Jesus Christ, you're unbelievable." I stand, my chair scraping against the marble floor. A few heads turn at nearby tables, but I couldn't care less.

"Ryan, please sit down," Erika pleads.

"It's obvious we're done here."

The walk through the restaurant feels endless. Waiters dodge my path, members stare, but all I hear is my heartbeat in my ears. It's not until I'm in the taxi that I realize my hands are shaking. What the hell happened? She didn't even flinch. Is she calling my bluff, thinking I won't sue? And Erika—her silence said everything. She knew nothing about the guardianship, that much was clear from her reaction. But instead of standing up to our grandmother, she fell back into her old role: the passive observer, stirring her tea while the family imploded. When I get back to Leo's apartment, he's already pouring two shots of mezcal. He sees my face.

"That bad, huh?"

"Worse." I drop onto his couch. "She didn't even pretend to care. I told her I knew about the guardianship, and she practically said nothing."

"What are you doing, then?"

"I don't know. I can sue her, for sure. Maybe I can make some noise in the art world."

"You could." Leo pours another round. "I can hook you up with a judge, but those motherfuckers are greedy. If I were you, I'd make noise first."

"How can I do that?"

"Let me ask around. We can probably find a renowned journalist or the owner of a news outlet. El Universal or El Nacional would be great. If not, an outlet with massive Instagram followers will do. One story about how she manipulated to steal from her grieving grandson? There's a story there."

"You're right."

Leo's phone buzzes. After checking it, he grabs his keys. "I have to run to a meeting. But think about it—your grandmother spent decades building her reputation."

I stay on the couch after he leaves, the mezcal settling warm in my stomach. I stare at the city lights coming alive through the window. My mother used to say every painting tells two stories—the one you see and the one hiding underneath. Maybe Leo's right. I can do both: the Diamantina money's coming in. Damn it, this is about to turn into a shitshow.

Chapter 10

"You have to come now," Leo texts.

"Where?"

"Trio, grab a cab."

Trio, or "threesome" in English, is a popular strip club in Caracas where anything goes—no questions asked. It's legal; no one asks questions. I've never been, but Leo's told me about it. You can smoke inside, and the security guards even hook you up with coke—for an upcharge, of course, but they solve your problem. With nothing else to do, I decide to go, but not before downing three mezcal shots to get in the right vibe.

The scene pulses with raw, vibrant energy as I enter. Past the leather-clad walls, a black marble bar stretches across the room, lined with girls in various states of boredom and anticipation. Velvet and red lights illuminate the floors. The metallic sheen of the pole highlights a stage that serves as the middle ground between the bar and the tables. Tables rise in tiers like a coliseum around the stage. Leo's at the biggest table, a booth tucked into the corner. Everyone's smoking and doing lines of cocaine at their tables—business as usual, I guess.

"Ryan, come here!" Leo yells. "I wanted to hook you up with this guy; he'll get you a meeting with a judge. He's from the First Instance of the Agrarian Court—different industry, but he can push the sentence through."

"Hermano, how you doing? Nice to meet you."

"All good. Come by tomorrow after lunch, and we'll sort it out."

A girl sits on my lap. "Hey, baby, we have a special today. We can go upstairs with a friend of mine for three hundred fifty dollars. One hour." She's a blonde with huge breasts and freckles on her chest. If I stuck my tongue out, I could practically lick her bra. How do I say no to that?

Leo overhears. "I got you, my man, no worries. Go have fun."

She grabs my hand. A petite, dark-haired girl stands at the bar, watching us. I grab her hand, and we head upstairs. As we climb, the threads reflect perfectly. Marbled stones hang from the ceiling, slightly covering the railings. On the second floor, we wait for a security guard to clear us. Music from downstairs pulses through the floor—a beat just beneath our feet. Inside, the room is surprisingly clean and modern—all black surfaces and dim lighting. A king-size bed and a jacuzzi that could easily fit five people dominate the space. Flanked by mirrored ceilings, dim lights travel through the glass door holding the shower on the other side. The dark-haired girl immediately starts preparing lines on a small glass table while the blonde pulls me toward the bed. She scoops a bump straight from the bag with her long-nailed pinky and holds it under my nose.

"Tranquilo, papi," she whispers in my ear.

The dark-haired girl joins us. Their hands are everywhere, and I let myself drift into the sensation, knowing that for the next hour, nothing else matters. But even as I surrender, a small voice in my head—one that sounds suspiciously like Elizabeth—whispers that I'm just following my usual pattern, seeking connection in all the wrong places. I push it away, drinking straight from the whiskey bottle next to me. One of them opens a condom and puts it in her mouth, rolling it onto me. I close my eyes and let the blur transform into a pleasant haze. Everything feels disconnected, like I'm watching myself from above. Is this what I've become—running from confrontation into these moments of artificial intimacy? My phone buzzes. It's Leo:

"Where you at, brother?"

I ignore it, pour a proper glass of whiskey and soda. The room spins slightly. The blonde whispers something in Spanish that makes the dark-haired girl laugh. Their performative intimacy should feel hollow, but right now, it's exactly what I need—no expectations, no complications, no morning-after regrets. The room's phone rings, and a security guard says time's up. I convince him for another hour, paying, of course. Time becomes fluid, marked only by ice cubes clinking against glass and the steady bass from downstairs. The lesbian porn on the TV inspires the girls to put on a show. We hop in the jacuzzi. Another message from Leo flashes on my phone. I text back: "Dude, I'm staying here a bit longer. I'll grab a cab, no worries."

"Okay," he replies.

The second hour flies by, and a security guard knocks, saying time's up. I glance at my phone—it's 3:00 a.m.

"When do you finish your shift?" I ask the blonde.

"I'm about to finish. Want to go somewhere else?"

"Sure."

The three of us pile into a cab with a sketchy driver who seems like he wants in on the action. The blonde gives directions, and we head west—not the best choice, but I'm so high and drunk I just go with it. We're taking bumps in the back when a sign of karma stops us. A sign against hedonism pulls us over—an alcabala, or police roadblock, on a dark street with few open businesses. At 4:00 a.m., nothing good can come of this. Cocaine clouds my rationality, and hours ago, I was with a judge, so I think these cops are small-time. I refuse to bribe them, and things get intense. They pull us out of the car and let the taxi go. I couldn't be madder.

"Look, I know these are prostitutes, and you have drugs. Hand them over."

"I was just with a judge; in fact, I'm meeting him later today. Want me to call him?" The cop searches the girls' purses and finds the drugs. "This won't be cheap," he says.

"Whatever," I reply.

Another cop, not liking my attitude, pushes me against the patrol car and searches me. Finding nothing, he handcuffs me. The blonde screams, "Just give them money; that's all they want!"

"He had his chance. You're coming with me to El Helicoide."

El Helicoide is a massive, spiraling architectural monstrosity in Caracas, never fully finished. Originally intended as Latin America's most modern commercial center in the sixties, it now serves as a brutal political prison. SEBIN, Venezuela's primary intelligence agency, operates it with a notorious reputation for detention and interrogation. The National Bolivarian Police, who lifted me, run a small section. We enter a small hall with no floor tiles—just dirt—and two cells at the end. Before the cells, a cement breakfast table hosts cops chatting, with six other detainees sitting on cement blocks in front of them.

The girls go straight to a cell, and they sit me on the dirt. The situation spirals beyond my control. My phone's dead, cutting off my lifeline. My mind races through legal justifications—I wasn't driving; the drugs weren't on me—but in El Helicoide, legality means little. This is a waiting game, and they expect me to crack. I won't. Time drags, and people around me are anxious.

Some talk about a five-thousand-dollar bribe to get out. That's nuts. A shift change brings new cops. One, with a show-off attitude, demands the girls' shoelaces—standard procedure, I guess. His insistence turns casual theft into a standoff. Two men, inches apart, escalate until someone fetches a superior. In less than a minute, a guy in his twenties storms in—baseball cap, red stamped shirt, torn jeans, Air Jordans. Without looking up, he finishes texting and barks:

"Firme! To the right!" Both cops snap to attention, hands behind backs. "What's the fucking problem with the shoelaces?"

Silently, a cop places the shoelaces on the table. "Miss, the shoelaces will stay here and be returned if you get out." That single "if" cuts through my drug-addled confidence. Where the fuck am I? What is this world? The boss signals me to the hallway.

"Listen, catire," he says, leaning close, "you gotta play ball if you want out. After twelve hours, I send you to a standard prison for processing. That's not where you want to be."

"Check my wallet. I've got no cash. Charge my phone, and we can work something out."

He searches through my wallet, finding the ZODI card. His expression shifts.

"What's this? Explain," he says, tapping the card.

"She's my mother's friend—the one who can bring money ASAP," I say naively.

"Are you crazy? No." He pauses, disgruntled. "Stay put."

Another cop approaches, removing my handcuffs with newfound respect—or fear. He pulls out a phone, starts recording, and asks, "Were you harmed during the procedure?"

"No."

"Did the cops follow procedure at every step of the detainment?"

Wanting to say "I guess," I answer, "Yes."

He nods, stops recording, and releases me within seconds. Outside, the morning sun hits like an accusation. It's probably noon. My phone's still dead, and a taxi driver lounging against his car sees me emerge.

"Where to?" he asks, not mentioning his rate. He knows I'll pay whatever.

"Las Mercedes," I say, climbing in. The leather seats stick to my sweat-soaked shirt. As we drive, I check my pockets—they've returned everything except some cash and, oddly, my belt. Small price for freedom. My mind drifts to the missed meeting with the judge. After a night in El Helicoide, taking on my grandmother doesn't seem so daunting. Maybe that's the lesson—sometimes you face real monsters to realize which fights matter. My phone comes to life as I plug it in at Leo's apartment. Messages flood in—missed calls from Leo, miscellaneous texts, and an email from Eric. A message from my aunt catches my eye: "Ryan, where are you staying? I have a gift for you."

As I stare at the Ávila, memories of my father's red helicopter return. He rented it to woo clients. I was about fifteen when he said, "You're old enough." On the way to the heliport, ten minutes outside Caracas, he laid out his plan: "I need to close these two clients. There's a waterfall in the mountains, and I've arranged for us to go. Two girls are already there; I just have to entertain these guys." The chopper sliced through the air, revealing the Ávila's countless secrets—the majestic mountain surrounding the Valley of Caracas. We landed near a clearing, a five-minute trail hike from the waterfall. Everything was staged perfectly: a waiter serving drinks, a cooler with whiskey and champagne, two stunning women swimming in the spring water. How do you beat that? The Canadians' faces said it all—sure, they'd seen Niagara Falls, but this intimate paradise was something else. For two hours, this paradise was theirs. My father wasn't just selling diamonds but the fantasy of a world where anything's possible. For the first and only time, I watched him work his magic. The girls played their roles perfectly—laughing at the right moments, making the clients feel like kings. "The secret," he told me later, "isn't the diamonds. It's making them believe they belong in this world." Jesus, should I be doing something else with my life?

"Dude, what the hell happened last night?" Leo asks, snapping me out of my thoughts as he sits at the pool table next to me.

"You don't want to know. I'm just glad I'm alive."

"How'd the meeting with the judge go?"

"Not great. He wants fifty thousand dollars to rule in my favor if I sue my grandmother."

"That's a lot of dough. Why didn't you negotiate down?"

"He started at a hundred thousand, but he wasn't happy I changed the meeting."

"If you decide to do it, I can knock off at least twenty percent. I've got good news, though—I found someone at El Nacional who'll run the story."

"You give him a grand and the full story, and he'll blow that shit up everywhere."

"That's fucking amazing. Yeah, I'm doing that right away. I don't know if I'll have time to meet him personally—I'm leaving tomorrow."

"You'll figure it out," Leo says, pulling out his phone. "The journalist's name is Roberto Mendez. Here's his number."

I save the number, already crafting the story in my head. My phone buzzes—another message from my aunt: "Hey, I'm downstairs."

"I gotta go downstairs for a bit. Thanks, brother. Really."

"No worries."

I take the elevator down, thinking about how Leo's been the one constant in all this chaos. While everyone else represents some complicated part of my past, he's just Leo—the guy who'd bail me out when we were kids, now helping me with this. He doesn't press for details; he just wants to help. What a great guy. The elevator doors open to the lobby. Through the glass doors, I see my aunt standing outside beside an SUV, holding a black cylindrical case—the kind artists use for canvases. I know what it is before she speaks.

"I've wanted to give you this for years," she says, her voice softer than usual. "It's the painting that hung in my living room. I know things are complicated with your grandmother, but this belongs with you. Your mother would've wanted that."

I take the case, feeling its weight—physical and emotional. Inside is one of my mother's earlier works, from before everything fell apart. I remember staring at it for hours during those mandatory family visits.

"Thank you," I say, surprised by the emotion in my voice. For once, this feels genuine—no hidden agendas, no family politics, just an aunt trying to do right by her nephew. She hugs me quickly and gets back in her SUV, perhaps to avoid the moment's awkwardness. Back at Leo's apartment, I unroll just enough of the canvas to confirm what I remembered.

"Look what I got, bro!" I say, excited.

"Amazing, brother. Congratulations. Want a beer?"

"Of course, dude, but let's just hang today. I'm exhausted."

"Sure. Want to watch the new Nolan movie and get some food?"

We settle into his oversized leather couch, the painting propped against the wall. The movie starts with Nolan's signature intensity—ticking clocks, mounting tension. But halfway through, we're more interested in picking apart the technical aspects than following the plot.

"The sound design's insane," Leo comments during a tense scene.

"Yeah, but what's with Nolan and his time obsession? Every fucking movie."

"That's his thing, man, like Tarantino with feet," Leo laughs, crushing another beer can. We spend the next hour debating directors' signatures—Scorsese's tracking shots, Kubrick's symmetry, Wes Anderson's perfect centers.

"It's funny," I say, grabbing another beer, "all these directors have their trademarks—it's like Nolan's compelled to explain everything to death. Take Inception—amazing movie, but he adds a character just to explain the plot to the audience."

"Yeah, but that's why people love his movies," Leo argues. "He makes complex shit digestible. Look at Tenet—without explanation, that movie's unwatchable."

"That's different. Tenet needed explanation because the concept was nuts. But look at what Villeneuve did with Arrival—complex time concepts, but he trusts the audience to figure it out."

"Arrival's different," Leo says, stretching on the couch. "It's about feelings more than mechanics. You're supposed to be confused until it hits you emotionally."

We fall into comfortable silence as the movie plays. The sun has set over Caracas, painting the city in deep blues. I check my phone—early flight tomorrow. As I get up to sleep, Leo looks at me and says, "Cool shorts, bro." I smile, reassured by my purchase. "They're crazy comfortable." The unspoken bond between us makes me feel at ease with Leo. What a great guy.

Chapter 11

Despite minor setbacks, things seem to be falling into place. The journalist has all the information to develop the story. I've got a new painting of my mother's safely wrapped and the sale documents tucked in my bag. Even the Diamantina deal is one less thing to worry about.

All that's left is to meet the new lawyers and prepare the case against my grandmother. The flight attendant offers me a beer. Why not? When else would I pay ten dollars for a mediocre beer? It tastes like victory—or maybe just relief. A week in Caracas felt like stepping into a parallel universe where everything moved faster, burned brighter. Even getting locked up in El Helicoide seems almost funny now. The captain announces our descent into Miami. Through the window, the city spreads out like a neon circuit board, all straight lines and artificial light—so different from Caracas's organic chaos.

The Uber ride from the airport feels endless. All I want is a shower and my bed. The driver tries to make conversation, but he doesn't get it; I'm tired from my monosyllabic responses. I should've pressed quiet mode in the app. The apartment feels exactly as I left it.

I toss my bags onto the couch and jump in the shower. As I step out and walk toward the terrace, towel tucked around my waist, the world suddenly falls apart. It's not a gradual realization—it's like someone flipped a switch in my body. It hits like a physical blow. The wall where my mother's paintings hung is now a void, two pale rectangles haunting the space where they should be. Thousands of ants tingle through my arms as my chest tightens. The floor seems to tilt, and I brace myself against the wall. The first thing I see is a Wynwood sculpture, which I hurl at the TV. My fist connects with the wall before I realize I'm moving, leaving a dent in the pristine white surface. What the fuck is going on?

Through the red haze of anger, more questions flood in. How did they get in? The lock isn't damaged. And most importantly, who? Are there even cameras in this fucking building? I grab my phone and call the lobby. The security guard surveys the damage. "We need to file a police report."

"Yeah, no shit," I snap.

He eyes the shattered TV, the scattered debris. "They trashed the apartment too?"

"No. The living room's on me. But the paintings—someone took my paintings."

"I can check the security footage," he offers, still eyeing the dent in the wall. "But if the lock wasn't forced..."

"I know what you're thinking," I cut him off. "That it was someone with a key. That's exactly what I'm afraid of."

He pulls out his phone, probably to call the cops. I should be more worried about explaining the state of the apartment, but all I can think about are those empty spaces on the wall.

"Sir?" The guard's voice pulls me back. "The police are on their way."

I nod absently, my mind racing. The spare key on top of the doorframe. Okay, let's think about this. No way in hell some random person would find that key and take only two paintings. Several people know about the spare key, but why now? Why this moment? Off the top of my head, only Louis and Monica know about it. Louis would never steal from me, I think. And Monica—why would she? Is she having money problems? Why wouldn't she ask me? The other option is my grandmother, but how could she orchestrate this? Seems far-fetched. The police arrive thirty minutes later. Two officers in pressed blue uniforms scan the apartment with practiced indifference. The younger one takes notes while his partner, a heavyset woman with graying hair at her temples, asks the standard questions.

"And you said nothing else was taken?" she asks, eyeing the broken TV.

"No, just the paintings. They belonged to my mother."

"Your mother's paintings?" She studies me more carefully. "Are they valuable?"

"Yes, very." I watch her expression shift from routine investigation to genuine interest.

"Are they insured?"

"No." I guess they asked to rule me out as a suspect.

"Any security cameras in the hallway?" she asks the guard.

"No, but there's one in the lobby."

"Okay, we'll need footage from that and any other cameras in the building." She turns to me.

"We'll need photos of the paintings, any documentation of ownership, and an estimated value. Also, a list of anyone who might've had access to your apartment."

I hesitate to give Monica's name. Do I really think she did it? Even considering her involvement feels like a betrayal, but what choice do I have? If I don't mention her and she's involved, the cops will never find the paintings. Besides, if she's innocent, what's the harm in checking?

"My cousin Louis has a spare key," I start, buying time. "And there's this girl I've been seeing—Monica."

"Do they have last names, or are they like Seal?" I glare at the cop's sarcasm, though it's kind of funny. I clarify their last names and stress that I'm in shock.

"Do they have a spare key?"

"No. If they're staying at my place, I leave the spare key on top of the doorframe. I was out of the country, so I didn't leave it out."

"Okay. We'll check the security cameras and get back to you."

The officer jots down both names without reaction—just another detail in another case. The door clicks shut behind them, leaving me alone with those empty spaces on the wall, each pale rectangle like a wound that won't heal. My phone buzzes around midnight. Monica's name flashes on the screen. Before I can answer, aggressive knocking echoes through the apartment.

"What the fuck is wrong with you?" She storms past me. "The cops came to my work, asking questions in front of everybody. You think I stole from you?"

"Monica, I—"

"No, shut up." She spins to face me. "Do you know how that looks? My boss was there. Jesus, Ryan. I let you in, and the first thing you do is throw me to the cops?"

"What was I supposed to do?" I shoot back. "I didn't say it was you. I only said you sometimes let yourself in. Someone with a key took them."

"Yeah, and you thought of me? The junkie whore who probably needed a fix?" Her laugh is bitter. "You know what's funny? I actually cared about you, despite all your shit." Her tone softens. "I didn't take your paintings, but I'm glad they're gone. Maybe now you'll face whatever you've been running from."

The door slams behind her. In the silence, I realize two things: first, she's telling the truth—she didn't take them. Second, I just lost something more valuable than the paintings. The situation with Monica weirdly clears my head. I grab my phone and scroll through recent calls. Louis's name catches my eye. Something about his last messages seems off now. Why was he so interested in when I was leaving for Venezuela? That fat fuck. I bet it was him. Unable to sleep, I decide to dig in. If this asshole took them, he probably talked to someone at MoMA, maybe through Carlos. The laptop screen burns my eyes as I dive deeper into the rabbit hole. MoMA's website is a maze of senior staff, officers, trustees, and curatorial departments. There's politics to all this. Curators don't just pick art they like—they navigate a web of donors, board members, and cultural movements. Every exhibition is years in the making, planned through committees and approved by multiple departments. No way I can get in touch with anyone here, not even by going to New York. My mother's name yields no results in their database. If there were real plans to exhibit her work, there'd be something. I fall asleep feeling defeated.

The next day brings no news. Elizabeth hasn't returned my calls. The officer said they still haven't checked the footage. I don't feel like talking to anyone. Do I really have no one now? Should I burden Leo with more of my problems? Call my uncle and tell him his fat bastard son stole my paintings?

I stare at the empty spaces on my wall until my vision blurs. The apartment walls feel like they're closing in. Monica's gone. The paintings are gone.

Even the cops seem to have filed this under "rich kid problems." I need to move. I need to breathe. An overwhelming wave of anger surges through my veins. I think of escaping, as I always imagine but never do. For some, escaping is boarding a plane to the other side of the world. For enlightened others, it's disconnecting into nothingness through meditation. For me, right now, it's getting on my kayak and paddling away. I feel no excitement as I walk the wooden plankway—just a desire to leave it all behind. I head north, where the canals and manatees are, and potentially hungry killing machines—crocodiles. Maybe one will eat me and end this madness.

After an hour of paddling, my back aches. I'm near a canal entrance, so I'll swim for a bit, then enter the canal. I jump ship, forgetting what my father told me—never leave a boat without a rope. A minute later, I realize the kayak is drifting fast with the wind. No time to waste; I swim to grab it. I stretch my right arm as far as I can and reach it. I didn't factor in the wind speed or my fifteen previous shoulder dislocations. A gust pushes the kayak, and the worst happens—my shoulder pops out in open water. If you don't know what a dislocated shoulder feels like, besides excruciating pain, the arm becomes useless. A friend taught me to pop it back by flexing my knee and grabbing my toe with the dislocated arm's hand. Of course, I have to do this underwater, thanks to my brilliant no-life-jacket policy. So, a dilemma hits me: pop it back or swim one-armed toward my blue kayak?

Two things are going for me right now. First, no boats are sailing through the bridge behind me. Second, the kayak is still relatively close. But the current is strong—every five seconds, the kayak moves about two yards, I'd guess. Instinctively, I swim one-armed toward it. It doesn't take long to realize the kayak's getting farther away. I don't particularly like Katy Perry, and I don't know why "Roar" is playing in my head. As the lyrics "you're gonna hear me roar" fade, I decide to pop my shoulder back into its socket. Luckily, it works on the first try.

Yes, I fucking did it. After a minute of desperate one-armed swimming, I hate Katy Perry. But now I'm feeling it. Oh yes, I'm roaring. Not the best choice to swim full speed, but I'm doing it. I'm gonna reach that kayak. Not more than a foot away, it happens again. Damn it. Okay, no worries, I'll pop it back. That would've been great. After ten tries and several screams, I revert to my failed one-arm swimming plan. A couple of minutes later, I don't hear "Roar" or any song. I can barely see the kayak now. I've never screamed so loud in my life, directing all my rage at Katy Perry, God, Louis, my grandmother—everyone.

A mile from shore, after half an hour of floating, two boats appear in the distance. My heart jumps. The first, a white center console, speeds by despite my screams. I wave my good arm frantically as the second—a slower fishing boat—approaches. It's still far; I can barely see people on deck. Of course, no one sees me. The sun's brutal now. I float on my back, conserving energy, letting the current take me. Funny how fighting something makes it worse. The pain in my shoulder is a dull throb, almost peaceful, like my body's given up sending warning signals.

The shoreline creeps into focus in slow motion. Unfamiliar buildings appear—I've drifted far east of the bridge. Time loses meaning. When my feet touch bottom, slick algae squishes between my toes. I stumble forward, plant both feet, and break into a desperate run. All I can do is laugh. I wave down a cab, thinking: yesterday was a shitty day, but somehow this one almost tops it.

Chapter 12

A couple of days pass, and the police finally call. I head to the station to meet Detective Garcia.

"Thanks for coming in," Garcia says, motioning me to sit. Her desk is cluttered with case files and empty coffee cups. "We've reviewed all the security footage."

"And?" She turns her monitor toward me.

"At 3:47 p.m. a week ago, a black Toyota Camry pulled into the valet section." She clicks through frames showing a man in dark clothes and a baseball cap emerging from the driver's side. "The subject knew exactly where to go— took the auxiliary service corridor instead of the main entrance." I lean forward, studying the grainy footage.

"Did you get a clear shot of his face?"

"Not from the parking cameras. But..." She switches to another feed. "We got this from the hallway camera on the service level. In the lobby footage, he keeps his head down and angled away from the cameras—clearly familiar with their placement. Timestamps show him entering your floor empty-handed at 3:52 p.m., then leaving ten minutes later with a partially filled black duffel bag." She closes the video window. "This wasn't random. The perpetrator knew the building's layout, knew the cameras' locations, and avoided most of them. This was professional."

Professional. The word hits like a punch. Was this Louis and my grandmother? Jesus.

"The car's plates were stolen," Garcia continues. "We're checking nearby traffic cameras, trying to track its route before and after. But honestly? This kind of precision—usually means someone hired it out." The theft feels different now—more calculated, more personal.

"So, what's next? Do you have a match for the guy?"

"We're looking for him. His name's Roger Aldana, mid-thirties, Venezuelan national, came to Miami five years ago. He's got a record in Caracas—mostly high-end burglaries."

"I already know who hired him. I just need to know why my cousin would do this. It doesn't make sense. I was in Caracas fighting with my grandmother over these exact paintings. She wanted to buy them to complete a collection worth over a million dollars that she's selling to a private collector. I refused, and now, a week after I'm back, they mysteriously disappear? My cousin Louis knew exactly when I was leaving for Venezuela. He's been to my place dozens of times—probably copied my key without me noticing." Garcia leans forward, suddenly more interested. "That's quite an accusation. Any proof connecting your cousin to Aldana?"

"Not right now."

"What does your cousin do?"

"He's in banking in New York City."

"Commercial banking, investment banking...?"

"I'd have to check. I think he's a broker."

"A broker in New York City? I'm sure he's making money. Why would he be involved?" she asks incredulously.

"That's what I don't know. Can you call someone in the NYPD to look into it? With my two pieces, the collection could be at MoMA. Maybe he's trying to find a buyer in New York. He had access to my apartment key a week before I left."

"I'll be honest. Given the nature of the crime, a joint operation with the NYPD is unlikely. If we traced Aldana to New York, maybe we could use an interstate communication platform to see who takes the case. Or if there's evidence connecting your cousin to Aldana—but right now, there's nothing I can do."

"So, what am I supposed to do? Just wait?"

Garcia sighs, her professional demeanor softening. "I understand your frustration. Right now, Aldana's our best lead. These guys have patterns, favorite spots to fence valuable items. We'll watch those channels."

As frustrating as it is not to find a link to my cousin, at least there's progress. Standing up, I feel a sudden shift in mood. I have my appointment with Elizabeth. After a week of trying to reach her, she finally answered. I've been thinking about this session more than I'd like to admit—something about her way of cutting through my defenses while making me feel understood. The afternoon sun casts long shadows across Brickell as I head to her building. The Mediterranean complex feels different today—quieter, more intimate. When I reach her office, Elizabeth opens the door herself. She's wearing a deep blue dress that makes her eyes look almost electric.

"You look exhausted," she says, studying my face with genuine concern.

"That obvious, huh?" I manage a weak smile.

"Come in." She steps aside, and I catch the faint scent of her perfume—something subtle and expensive. The office feels different, warmer somehow. She's moved the chairs closer, eliminating the usual therapeutic distance.

"I tried reaching you," I say, settling into my chair.

"I know." Her voice blends professional distance with intimate understanding. "Sometimes we need space to process things on our own." I pause; something about her response doesn't sit right. How would she know what I needed? I haven't spoken to her since before Venezuela. The thought slips away as she leans forward slightly, her presence drawing me back.

"Tell me about Venezuela," she says.

"It was weird, like a parallel universe. If it wasn't for Leo, I wouldn't have done anything. And you, for that matter—our last talk made me think a lot. These sessions ground me."

She smiles, a gentle expression that warms the room. "And what did you think about?"

"What you said about patterns." I lean forward, drawn into her pull. "How maybe I'm not just running from my past but from anything real. Anyone real." Elizabeth's eyes hold mine a moment longer than professional.

"And what feels real to you now, Ryan?"

The question hits deeper than it should. The setting sun paints her profile in amber light, and I'm struck by how familiar she feels. "I don't know anymore," I admit. "Everything I thought was solid just... disappeared. The paintings, Monica, even my relationship with Louis. Sometimes I think these sessions are the only constant I have left."

"And that scares you?" she asks softly.

"Shouldn't it?" I shift, suddenly aware of how much I've revealed. "My mother's paintings were the one thing I thought no one could take. Now they're gone, and I'm sitting here talking about feelings while someone's probably arranging their sale."

"You're angry," she observes, her voice blending empathy and professional distance.

"I'm tired," I correct. "Tired of losing things. Tired of not trusting anyone." The words slip out: "Except you, I guess." She leans forward, close enough that I catch her perfume again. Her eyes search mine with an intensity that blurs professional boundaries. "Trust is earned, Ryan. Even with yourself." Her voice drops, intimate. "Especially with yourself." I shift, my shoulder protesting. The moment stretches, heavy with unspoken possibilities. Elizabeth notices. "You're in pain?"

"Just a shoulder thing. Old injury." Her patient silence makes me continue. "Actually, I almost died yesterday. Lost my kayak, dislocated my shoulder, and swam for what felt like hours."

"What were you trying to escape?" she asks, cutting to the core—not "what happened" or "are you okay."

"Everything. Nothing." I let out a bitter laugh. "Maybe just myself." Her expression softens, but there's a knowing look in her eyes, as if she sees more than I'm saying. "Sometimes we need to lose control to find ourselves."

"Yeah, well, it clearly didn't work."

She studies me, her presence comforting yet unnerving. "The paintings, the kayak, the relationships you push away—they're about control, aren't they? Holding onto something solid when everything feels like water slipping through your fingers." Her hand moves toward mine on the armrest, then withdraws. "Our time's up, Ryan. Think about what you're really afraid of losing." Walking to my car, my phone buzzes. The *El Nacional* article is live:

LEGAL BATTLE BREWS OVER LATE ARTIST'S MILLION-DOLLAR COLLECTION

By Roberto Mendez, El Nacional

In what appears to be a carefully orchestrated legal maneuver spanning fifteen years, prominent Caracas socialite Elisa Torres de Montero has maintained control over her deceased daughter's artistic legacy through a controversial guardianship arrangement, an *El Nacional* investigation has revealed. Documents obtained by this newspaper show that following the tragic death of renowned artist Camila Torres in 2010, Montero secured legal guardianship over her then-teenage grandson, Ryan Torres, citing psychological trauma.

This guardianship, unusually maintained into his adulthood through an interdiction sentence, gave Montero control over Torres's entire body of work. The revelation comes amid growing interest in

Torres's final collection, *Resplandor Interior*, recently discovered in a Caracas studio apartment. Art experts value the complete collection at over $1.2 million USD. Sources indicate the collection is being prepared for private sale, despite interest from major institutions, including New York's Museum of Modern Art.

"The legal mechanisms employed here raise serious ethical concerns," says Dr. Manuel Rivas, an expert in Venezuelan estate law. "Maintaining guardianship over an adult residing in the United States, without documented ongoing interaction, appears to circumvent standard legal protocols."

The story has sent shock waves through Caracas's art community, where Torres's work has seen substantial appreciation. "Camila Torres's final collection represents a pivotal moment in Venezuelan contemporary art," notes curator Isabella Márquez. "Its sale to a private collector would be a significant loss to the public sphere."

Multiple attempts to reach Montero for comment were unsuccessful. Her grandson, now a Miami resident, possessed two crucial pieces of the collection, without which its value diminishes considerably. However, in a dramatic development just before publication, sources confirm these paintings were stolen from his Miami apartment last week. The Miami-Dade Police Department has identified a Venezuelan national as a person of interest in the theft, raising questions about potential connections to the ongoing family dispute.

"This case exemplifies how legal instruments meant to protect vulnerable individuals can be manipulated to control valuable artistic estates," Rivas adds. "The implications extend far beyond this single collection."

Chapter 13

My phone rings at 8:00 a.m. Erika's name flashes on the screen, and for a moment, I consider letting it go to voicemail. But something in me wants to hear the chaos I've created.

"Ryan, she's furious," Erika says, her voice trembling. "She's been up all night calling everyone—lawyers, friends on the museum board, everyone."

"So, what do you want me to do? The article's already out."

"She's threatening to expose things about your father's business dealings. Says if you want to play dirty—"

"My father's been dead for fifteen years." A call beeps through—private number. "I have to go."

"Ryan, please, just—"

I switch lines. For a moment, there's only silence, then: "Was this really necessary?" My grandmother's voice, cold and precise as I remember it. "Dragging my name through the mud like some common criminal?" I stay silent, not wanting to respond.

"You have no idea what you're doing." Her tone shifts slightly—not quite concern, but close. "There are things you don't understand about your mother's work, about what we're trying to protect."

"You fucked me over for years, and now what? Want to explain my reaction? Talk to my lawyer from now on."

I hang up before she can respond. Her words echo—things you don't understand about your mother's work. Classic manipulation, dangling information like bait. My phone buzzes again—Erika. I silence it and pour coffee.

The call with the Caracas lawyers feels like a scene from a bad movie—two serious faces crammed into my laptop screen, taking turns explaining why this case is "complicated." The senior partner outlines our options: challenge the guardianship directly, file for damages over the apartment sale, or pursue both. Without proof of ongoing interaction with my grandmother over the past fifteen years, the guardianship might strengthen my case—showing she failed to establish contact for proper guidance. They estimate at least six months before any movement. Following Eric's advice, I request a draft lawsuit to question the guardianship and for them to represent me in court, asking for a cost estimate.

Carlos calls right after. What starts as his usual diplomatic bullshit turns into something else—he reveals something that makes me think. My grandmother has been selling my mother's paintings through various channels, with Carlos as one of them. He deduces she must not have many left, meaning she's likely desperate for money. She may be many things, but she cares about my mother's art—or did, before. Maintaining appearances now trumps preserving her daughter's legacy. The irony doesn't escape me. For people like my grandmother, status isn't just wealth or power—it's identity itself. Strip away the mansion, the social connections, the carefully curated image of cultural authority, and what's left? She's spent decades building herself around her societal position, each charity gala and museum board appointment another brick in the wall between her true self and the world.

To maintain that facade, she'll sacrifice anything—even my mother's art, the very thing that gave her cultural legitimacy. In her world, appearance isn't just more important than reality—it is reality. The whispers at the Country Club, the social alliances, the perfect image of the family matriarch preserving her daughter's legacy—that's more real to her than the paintings she's selling off piece by piece. Well, fuck her.

Something about Carlos's sudden honesty doesn't add up. He talks about each sale like he's keeping score. A pattern emerges: Louis knew exactly when I'd be in Venezuela, probably timed the theft to the hour. The MoMA story is perfect cover—get the paintings "discovered," build buzz through institutional validation, then flip them to private collectors for serious money. My cousin must be more desperate than his Wall Street facade suggests. Everyone gets their cut: my grandmother maintains her social standing, Carlos gets his broker fees, and Louis—whatever hole he's trying to fill must be deep enough to make betraying family worth it. The thought of him calculating the price of our relationship, weighing it against what they promised him, makes me want to throw up. But why would Carlos reveal so much about my grandmother?

The *Miami Herald* article lands like a bomb two days later. My phone buzzes at 6:00 a.m.—first with a text from Eric, then a flood of notifications as the story spreads to art blogs and local news:

G. A. Guzman

MIAMI ART THEFT LINKED TO FAMILY DISPUTE OVER MILLION-DOLLAR COLLECTION

By Sarah Chen, Miami Herald

The recent theft of two paintings from a Miami apartment has unveiled a complex web of family drama and high-stakes art world maneuvering, the *Miami Herald* has learned. The paintings, part of renowned Venezuelan artist Camila Torres's final collection, were stolen from her son's Brickell apartment last week. Sources close to the investigation confirm that a professional art thief, identified as Roger Aldana, was caught on security footage entering the building.

The theft comes as Torres's work gains unprecedented attention in international art circles. Several major institutions have expressed interest in the complete *Resplandor Interior* collection, with experts suggesting institutional recognition could significantly impact its market value.

The missing paintings' owner, Ryan Torres, recently went public with allegations that his grandmother, prominent Caracas socialite Elisa Torres de Montero, has maintained illegal control over his mother's estate through questionable legal mechanisms. The story first broke in Venezuela's *El Nacional*, raising questions about the intersection of family inheritance and art world politics.

"This case highlights the unique challenges in protecting artist estates, especially when family dynamics and international borders are involved," says Dr. Maria Suarez, professor of art law at the University of Miami. "The timing of the theft, just as the collection's profile is rising, raises serious concerns."

Detective Sandra Garcia of the Miami-Dade Police Department confirms an active investigation but declined to comment on potential suspects. Sources familiar with the case suggest the paintings may have already left Florida, possibly bound for New York.

Notifications flood in. One from my boss stands out—show up tomorrow or don't bother coming back. Then Elizabeth: "You must be going through hell right now, Ryan. Let's talk ASAP; I can move some stuff around." Before I can answer, Eric calls. We talk for a while as I update him on the situation. After hanging up, I stare at the painting my aunt Erika gave me. I hung it where the stolen ones used to be—maybe out of spite, maybe to fill the void. The more I look, the more I see something familiar in the brushstrokes. My mother always said you could read an artist's state of mind through their technique. These strokes are angry, almost violent, like she was fighting the canvas itself. The colors bleed into each other, creating shapes that seem to move if you stare too long. My eyes grow heavy as I try to decode what she was saying... A knock at the door jolts me awake.

The sun has shifted, casting different shadows. Through the peephole, I see Elizabeth, still in work clothes but with her hair down. This can't be good. I open the door but freeze, processing that my therapist is here. Elizabeth shifts uncomfortably, probably realizing how far we've crossed professional boundaries.

"I saw the article," she says, her voice softer than in her office. Before I can respond, she walks past me. Her perfume catches me off guard—nothing like her usual scent. "You haven't been answering your phone."

"Wait, can we stop for a second? What are you doing here?" The words come out harsher than intended. She turns, something shifting in her expression. "You're right. This is completely inappropriate." She runs a hand through her hair, a gesture I've never seen in her office. "I left him two days ago. He was cheating on me."

"Okay. By 'him,' you mean your husband I've never met. So, are we friends now?"

"Why are men so difficult? Do you want me to leave, or are you pouring me a drink?" I can't argue with that reasoning. I grab a silver tequila bottle and two shot glasses from the freezer. The soft ice on the pyramidal bottle makes it even more appealing. As I pour,

Elizabeth wanders the apartment. "I love your apartment." Her gaze locks onto my mother's painting. "This is intense. Your mother's, I assume?"

"Yes, I just got it." I hand her a shot, trying not to notice how different she looks outside her office—more real. "My aunt Erika gave it to me after the others were stolen."

"The technique's fascinating—almost violent." She takes the shot. "Like she's trying to break through something." I study the painting, struck by how she sees what I saw. Before I can respond, she moves to the couch, kicking off her heels with surprising casualness. "So, lay it on me. What's going on?"

Something about her sitting there, feet tucked under, glass in hand, feels surreal—my therapist discussing my case like old friends. And, clearly, hitting on me. I summarize my theories, making exceptional sense. She nods, staring at me sensually—or so I perceive it. The sexual tension builds; we both know why she's here. She's waiting for me to make a move. But insecurity and indecision creep in. Throwing myself at her isn't my style—women don't like it.

A lawyer I dated years ago confirmed this; after dinner at her place, in a similar couch-drinking moment, I said, "So, should we just..." and made a kissing gesture with my index fingers. Should I try this proven approach? Hell yeah. Elizabeth laughs and leans in. I can't recall a more perfect kiss. Her lips are soft, tentative at first, then the kiss deepens. Her hand finds my neck, pulling me closer. The doctor-patient distance dissolves as she moves onto my lap. My hands trace her back, feeling the heat through her silk blouse. Time stretches and compresses, the world narrowing to her breath against my neck, her perfume's subtle scent, the way her body fits mine like we've done this a thousand times.

I pull her closer, hands tangling in her hair as she unbuttons my shirt. Her touch is electric, erasing every thought but the need for more. We stumble toward the bedroom, leaving a trail of clothes. The last daylight paints shadows across her skin as she pulls me onto the bed. Every movement feels inevitable, like we've been heading here since our first session. Her body arches against mine, and I lose myself in her heat, the taste of tequila on her lips, the way she whispers my name like a confession.

Her nails dig into my back as I kiss her neck. There's an urgency in her touch that matches mine—like we're both trying to forget everything outside this room. Professional boundaries, ethical lines, my grandmother's schemes, her failed marriage—it all fades against the rhythm of our bodies. When she comes, her body trembling, I'm about to follow, but she stops me, whispering to stay in and trust her. After that magical connection, I collapse beside her in a tangle of sheets and limbs.

I wake to sunlight streaming through the windows, Elizabeth facing me. We wake together, no awkward morning-after tension, no rushed gathering of clothes. She smiles, making my chest tight. In the morning light, she looks younger, more vulnerable.

"Coffee?" I ask.

"Please."

I slip out of bed, pulling on my favorite shorts. In the kitchen, I grind beans and watch steam rise from the machine, still processing last night. When I return with two mugs, she's lying in bed, looking at her phone. I hand her a cup.

"How's your day looking?"

"My day's packed—bunch of patients. You?"

"I gotta meet the cops; I'm running late, actually. There's an extra toothbrush if you want."

I grab my phone and jump into the shower, leaving the bathroom door open in case she gets the crazy idea to join me. The *Miami Herald* Instagram post has me hooked—so many comments. My gossip eagerness pulls me to take the phone into the shower, water running over it, probably fueling a new addiction.

"Are you seriously on your phone in the shower?" Elizabeth's voice makes me jump. She's by the sink in my T-shirt, toothbrush in hand, looking amused and concerned. "And I thought my patients had attachment issues."

"You lost therapist privileges when you got in my bed." I angle the phone away from the spray.

"Maybe, but anyone can see this is pathological." She brushes her teeth, watching me through the mirror.

"Give me that before you destroy it." She reaches into the shower and snatches the phone, her professional demeanor undermined by my shirt.

"You're gonna be late for your meeting." Watching her brush her teeth at my sink, wearing my shirt, giving me shit about my phone addiction—it feels weirdly normal. I like this couple dynamic. Did the perfect woman just walk into my apartment at exactly the right moment?

Chapter 14

"Hey, brother, did you talk to that judge?" I ask without preamble.

"Yeah, he's ready. I got him down to forty thousand; he wants twenty up front, the rest with the ruling. He'll also cut the lawsuit response time to three days. The lawyer's ready with the power of attorney," Leo responds.

"Fuck it, let's do it. I'll wire you today."

I hang up as I pull into the concrete building. *Miami Police Department* in big blue bold letters—somehow it reminds me of *RoboCop*. A burst of air conditioning hits as I push the heavy glass doors. The metal detector lady eyes me oddly. Am I being paranoid? The scent of coffee wafts from Detective

Garcia's desk at the hallway's end. Her expression says she doesn't have good news.

"We found Aldana," she says as we walk to a small interview room.

"That's good news, right?"

She sets a file on the table and gestures for me to sit. "Yes and no. He's talking, but it's a dead end. Says he was hired through a secure messaging app, paid in cryptocurrency, never met the client face-to-face."

"That sounds like bullshit."

"It's not," Garcia says, opening the case file. "These professional thieves have adapted. The app's called Ghost—end-to-end encryption, messages disappear after being read, no user verification. Our cyber unit's trying to crack it, but so far, nothing."

"What about the money? You can trace cryptocurrency, right?"

"In theory." She slides over a printout showing a web of transactions. "The payment was in Monero, not Bitcoin, designed to be untraceable. The funds bounced through dozens of wallets before reaching Aldana, each transfer obscuring the origin."

"So, we've got nothing?"

"Not quite." She pulls out another document. "Aldana doesn't know who hired him, but he knows his instructions. Your paintings were to be delivered to a specific storage facility in Miami. By the time we got there, they were gone, but we have security footage of the pickup."

"And?"

"The person who picked them up used fake credentials, but we're working on facial recognition. Plus, Aldana got specific instructions on handling the paintings—temperature control, no direct sunlight, specialized packing materials. This wasn't just any theft. Whoever's behind it knows art preservation."

A day passes in a blur of phone calls with lawyers and wire transfers to Leo. I haven't heard from Elizabeth since she left my apartment yesterday morning. I finally text her:

"Lunch today?"

Where should I take her? Nothing too fancy—impressing her isn't me anymore. Dinner's better, no rush from her hectic day. Somewhere like me, maybe a sports bar to hang out and watch a game. There's a good one in Brickell. We could order wings. No, fuck that, I suck at eating wings. She'd see me eat like a Neanderthal. Nobody should eat wings on a first date.

My boss messages again, reiterating what he made clear—show up tonight or don't come back. Part of me wants to tell him to go fuck himself, but practicality wins. With the Diamantina money, I'm safe for a while, but I need some kind of decent routine.

Elizabeth doesn't answer, and I head to the restaurant. The elevator doors open with their familiar sigh, releasing me into Friday afternoon pandemonium. The noise hits first—a tidal wave of voices, laughter, and clattering dishes. It's the happy chaos that pays the bills, but right now, it means I'm ten steps behind. My eyes sweep the room, a bartender's scan of the battlefield. Every table's a tiny island of animated conversation, mismatched wooden chairs pulled out at all angles. Along the far wall, plush low-backed booths overflow with tech bros celebrating, patrons melting into worn leather as they gesture and laugh. Intense sunlight filters through slatted panels lining the upper windows, striping the scene and highlighting dancing dust motes.

Instead of a ceiling, wooden slats curve overhead like an upturned ship's hull, creating a wave-like effect that feels both open and intimate. Oversized glass pendant lights hang like luminous raindrops, casting warm halos over the chaos. The place has that effortlessly cool Miami vibe—raw wood tables, worn leather, textured walls with trailing vines near the bar—stylish without pretension, where you can dress up or down and feel at home.

My gaze locks onto the bar, three deep with thirsty patrons. Mike's about to end his shift, and the prep area's a mess—a war zone of citrus peels and empty garnish trays. Bottles behind me shine under spotlights, most without pour spouts. Mike removes his apron, eyeing his exit.

"Seriously, bro? You're leaving it like this?" Mike glances at his phone, then at me. "I've got somewhere to be in thirty minutes. Can you help me out?"

"You always do this. I've got a full bar to manage, and you're leaving everything like shit."

"Look," Mike's voice tightens, "I covered your shifts last week on your 'vacation.'" His tone drips suggestion.

"Are you fucking serious? Did I ask you to? You were assigned those shifts. It's not like you didn't make money."

Mike steps closer, jaw tight. "You know your problem? You think you own this place." His finger jabs toward my chest. "Just because management lets you get away with your shit doesn't mean—"

"Get your finger out of my face." I grip a bottle opener, clenching a tight fist. The space between us vanishes.

"Or what?" Mike doesn't budge.

Conversations around us fade as the tension draws eyes. I step back, flashing a subtle smile to create space. Everything slows—the murmur of voices dies, ice settles in glasses, background music fades. My fist, weighted by the bottle opener, connects with his jaw before he reacts. Mike goes down hard, crashing into the prep station. Chaos erupts. Customers jump back, drinks spilling. Someone screams. Mike struggles up, blood trickling from his lip, knocking over bottles as he grabs for support. The crash of glass snaps everyone awake.

Juan, a busser, intercedes like a ghost. All five-foot-five of him, with his boyish face and faint mustache—the kid who shares his joint behind the dumpster after closing, dreaming of a food truck. He's sharp, sending money to his mother in Guadalajara. Started as a dishwasher three years ago, barely speaking English, now bussing tables. His food truck plan isn't just talk; he's got a business plan, recipes tested on staff. Mexican street food with a Miami twist. I know he's got my back.

"Tranquilo, tranquilo," Juan says, grabbing Mike. His eyes meet mine, serious, not the usual stoned grin from our late-night talks.

Mike backs off, fuming but reading the room. The manager bursts through the kitchen door.

"What the hell's going on?" I survey the mess—scattered glass, spilled drinks, customers filming. Something clicks.

"I'm sorry for hitting that douche, but I quit." The manager's face reddens, but I'm already walking. I toss my bar key on the counter, catching Juan's eye. He gives a slight nod.

Half the dining room didn't notice the show, too caught up in overpriced cocktails and Friday hype. I barely hear my boss's angry words as I reach the elevator. I check my phone—no response from Elizabeth. Maybe that's another chapter to rethink. The doors slide shut, and for the first time today, I can breathe.

I sit in my car, directionless. The clock reads 5:30 p.m. Elizabeth should finish soon. I'll visit her. In my experience, visiting women who don't text back is a horrible idea—the worst. But I've got nowhere to go. She's still my therapist, and I just made an impulsive, probably terrible mistake.

"I just saw the article. Are you okay?" Monica texts.

Elizabeth's overshadowed her these past days. The drive to the Brickell Medical Arts Building feels longer, traffic crawling as rush hour begins. What should I reply to Monica? She probably still hates me for how I treated her. Maybe I should focus on Elizabeth. Although, I shouldn't dump my problems on her yet. I pull into the parking lot, noticing a new sign: "COMING SOON: BRICKELL HEIGHTS LUXURY CONDOS." A rendering shows a glass tower replacing the current building. It must be recent—maybe why Elizabeth mentioned moving her practice. I note to ask where she's relocating. The Mediterranean complex looks different today. The entrance shows peeling paint, cracks in the stucco wider than last time. The courtyard fountain is dry, filled with dead leaves. Strange—it was running days ago.

Building 7 is at the far end, past empty storefronts with "FOR LEASE" signs. Unease grows as I reach the entrance. The lobby's directory has blank spaces where tenant names should be. I scan for "Elizabeth Silva, MD, PhD"—nothing. Maybe they're removing names for demolition. Beyond, the space is empty—not just unoccupied, but vacant. Dust sheets cover sparse furniture. Paint peels in long strips. The hallway feels narrower. Spiderwebs cling to the window from our sessions. "What the hell?" I mutter, stepping inside. My footsteps echo. This can't be right. We had a session here last week—the leather armchairs, bookshelves, the waiting room painting I studied on that comfortable sofa. None of it's here.

I scroll frantically for Elizabeth's contact. It's gone. Call history? Nothing. Messages? Nothing. Impossible—I texted her two hours ago. My heart pounds as I pace the empty room. Outside in the hall, rusty metal chairs replace the sofa. A faded rectangle on the wall marks where a painting hung—the one with ambiguous figures from the waiting room.

A shadow creeps in. Tingles in my arms turn to miniature nails pressing against me. I question everything. My breath comes in short gasps, catching like barbed wire. I press my palms to my temples, trying to ground myself. My phone feels heavy as I scroll through contacts again and again, each swipe more desperate. I sink to the floor, back against the wall. Dust makes me cough. I close my eyes, trying to picture Elizabeth's face, but it blurs like smoke. Her voice echoes distantly. Footsteps behind me make me stand up.

"Elizabeth?"

"What Elizabeth?" a man answers, looking like a gardener.

"Dr. Elizabeth—she has her office here."

"Maybe last year. This lot's been empty a while."

I lower my head, a smile turning into uncontrollable laughter. Viktor Frankl would call this normal. Something Elizabeth mentioned in session comes back to me—Frankl's observation about paradoxical reactions to extreme situations, the mind's attempt to shield itself from unbearable truth.

My laughter bounces off walls that never held the conversations I remember.

A ringing in my ears follows me to my car. Messages from my grandmother, likely about the lawsuit, make me want to hurl the phone out the window. The drive home blurs with red lights and horns. Why can't I control this rage and sadness? How much have I imagined? Is my life an elaborate delusion?

At my apartment, I head to the safe and grab the gun my father gave me. From the balcony, I stare at the horizon, right hand clutching the gun—a black Glock, second generation. Unlike a revolver, it has no safety, so my finger on the trigger, as now, allows no sudden moves.

A memory flashes—yesterday morning in the shower, phone in hand. I dropped it, cursed, picked it up myself, left it on the toilet. The bathroom empty, just me, talking to no one as water streamed down my face. Tears spill as I realize I'm absolutely alone. I've known since my parents died but never accepted it. I thought I'd find someone who understands or accepts me. No luck—so it's my fault. What am I doing here? I slowly raise the gun's barrel to my mouth, knowing it must be one immediate action. My last thought as I exhale: Are those weak who pull the trigger? I close my eyes and take the deepest breath I've ever taken.

Chapter 15

Three hard knocks to the front door make me open my eyes. "It's me, Monica, open up".

Suicide has always been of particular interest to me. Popular opinion is that people are weak for leaving all behind. I think is courageous as fuck to take your own life. You have to have some balls. Is it the easy way out of the problem? Fuck no. It's the perpetual way out. You are forfeiting any potential joy, new experience, smell, taste, hug, sight, feel everything. Because of what? Some problems you think have no solution. Which is almost always money.

The gun feels heavier now, like it's gained weight from absorbing my intention. Three more knocks, louder this time. Monica's voice cuts through my thoughts again—"Ryan, I know you're in there. Open the fucking door." I remain frozen, the cold metal still pressed against my lips. What would she find if she somehow got in? My body, my blood, the mess I'd leave behind. The knocking becomes pounding. "Ryan! I swear to God if you don't open this door..." Her voice sounds different than Elizabeth's—rougher, real.

I slowly lower the gun. Not because I want to live, but because some small, functioning part of my brain has latched onto a basic social protocol—you don't ignore someone at the door. Even when you're about to kill yourself. It's absurd, but it's enough to break the moment. I place the gun on the sofa, carefully, like I might need it again in a few minutes. The walk to the door feels endless, my legs moving through invisible resistance. I unlock the door and pull it open, not bothering to hide the tear tracks on my face or the emptiness I know is visible in my eyes.

Monica stands there, somehow both exactly as I remember and completely different. Her eyes widen slightly as she takes me in, her expression shifting from irritation to concern in an instant.

"Jesus, Ryan," she says, pushing past me into the apartment. "What the hell is going on? You haven't answered your phone in days."

Has it been days? Time feels slippery, unreliable. I close the door, turning to find her frozen in the middle of the living room, staring at the gun on the sofa.

"Were you—" she starts, then stops, her eyes moving from the gun to me. "Ryan?"

I don't answer—can't answer. The words stick in my throat like glass. Monica approaches and hugs me. I burst into tears, letting go. We stay like that for what feels like hours, her arms steady as sobs wrack my body. When I pull back, the room seems clearer somehow. Monica guides me to the couch, gently moving the gun aside like it's a dirty tissue.

"Talk to me," she says simply, her voice direct, no games or hidden meanings—the quality I've always loved.

"I think I'm losing my mind." The words come out raw. "There was this therapist..."

"Elizabeth?" Monica's eyes hold mine. "The one you mentioned at dinner?"

"What dinner?" I stare blankly.

"You told me about this amazing therapist who understood you, helped you see patterns in your relationships." She watches me carefully. A memory flickers—sitting across from Monica at a small table, candlelight catching her wine glass. But I thought that was with Elizabeth. Wasn't it?

"We talked about those things, Ryan—over coffee, at the beach that morning, during dinner," Monica says, gentle but firm. "You kept mentioning her, but when I asked for details—her full name, her office—you'd change the subject." My head spins as distorted Memories surface. The conversation about art and value I thought I had with Elizabeth—was that with Monica?

"I came over," Monica says quietly. "You were a mess about the article. We drank tequila, talked all night. But you kept slipping in and out."

My phone buzzes—a message from Leo: "Your grandmother got to the judge first. She offered double. I'm sorry, brother."

A month ago, this would've crushed me. Now I'm just tired. Monica's hand finds mine, warm and real—no professional distance, no careful therapeutic tone, just someone who sees me at my worst and stays. I look at my mother's painting, the one Erika gave me. The angry brushstrokes I analyzed seem different now—less violent, more passionate. My mother wasn't breaking the canvas; she was reaching out, connecting. Maybe that's all we're trying to do.

"It's fucked up," I say to Monica. "I made up this whole person when you were q here all along." Her hand tightens—no words, no analysis.

The sun's low, painting the apartment in orange shades. My mother's paintings could be anywhere—a New York gallery, a collector's vault, a storage unit. My grandmother will keep being herself; Louis, too. But none of that matters now. I've got Monica's hand, my mother's painting, and for the first time since my parents died, the ground feels solid.

"Don't leave," I manage to say. She pulls me closer.

"Not a chance."